WOLF BLOOD

Call of the Wild

ROBERT RIGBY

Piccadilly
PRESS

To Emily

First published in Great Britain in 2015 by
PICCADILLY PRESS
80–81 Wimpole St, London W1G 9RE
www.piccadillypress.co.uk

Text copyright © Piccadilly Press, 2015

Wolfblood copyright © BBC 2012 and ZDFE 2012

Based on the series created by Debbie Moon

A CIP catalogue record for this book is available
from the British Library.

ISBN: 978-1-84812-518-6
also available as an ebook

1

Typeset by Palimpsest Book Production Ltd, Falkirk, Stirlingshire

Printed and bound by Clays Ltd, St Ives Plc

FSC

Piccadilly Press supports the Forest Stewardship Council (FSC),
the leading international forest certification organisation, and is
committed to printing only on Greenpeace-approved
FSC-certified paper.

Piccadilly Press is an imprint of Bonnier Publishing Fiction,
a Bonnier Publishing company
www.bonnierpublishingfiction.co.uk
www.bonnierpublishing.co.uk

One

Snow lay thick on the ground as a lone wolf crested the frozen hilltop, running at full speed, desperately trying to stay clear of three howling, snarling pursuers.

The chase across the bleak moorland had been long and gruelling, and as the winter sun slipped down the sky and night approached, the three bigger and stronger wolves relentlessly closed on their younger target.

Close to exhaustion, the young wolf paused momentarily in the shadow of a tall tree to glance back towards his hunters, glimpsing their yellow eyes blazing through the misty gloom. There was no time to rest; this was life or death.

Stoneybridge Moor was gradually giving way to the beginnings of dense woodland, so the young wolf turned and plunged onwards into the trees.

Much deeper in the woodland nestled the centuries-old home of Maddy Smith and her parents, Emma and Daniel. The house was snug and comfortable, especially in winter, but tonight there were no thoughts of an evening snuggled cosily in the sitting room. They had completed the preparations for the coming night of the full moon and were making their way down ancient stone steps into the den. The den was comfortable too, in its own way – if you happened to be a wolf. It was more of an animal's lair than a room and had been cut into the solid rock beneath the house. There were rock shelves to lie on, a mud floor, and thick branches to claw.

The Smiths were Wolfbloods, and the silvery light of the full moon would see them transform from human form into wolves. Every instinct would then urge them to run wild, explore, hunt and roam freely across the moor and through the woodland.

But running wild as wolves meant danger and the threat of discovery, so every full moon, Daniel Smith led his family down into the den, where they remained in safety until daylight, when they returned to their human form.

They were in high spirits, though, and as playful as wolf cubs as they entered the den. In the everyday human world they were constantly aware that transformation had to be avoided, but on the night of the full moon it was inevitable. So despite the frustration of being locked in the cellar, the thrill of taking wolf form meant they were buzzing with energy and excitement.

Daniel locked the door and as he turned to continue chatting his head came into sharp contact with something wooden and heavy. 'Ow!'

Maddy and her mum couldn't stop themselves from laughing.

Daniel rubbed his head and glared at a large wooden owl hanging from the ceiling. 'Who put that thing there?'

'It's a present from Shannon,' Maddy said, stifling her laughter. 'Apparently it's the wise old owl of the forest, keeping a watchful eye on all Wolfbloods.'

The owl did appear to be watching them through huge, black glass eyes.

'It's horrible,' Daniel said, returning the owl's frozen stare.

'Shannon just wants to be part of things, Dad,' Maddy said. 'Tom does too. They want to help if they can.'

Shannon Kelly and Tom Okanawe were Maddy's best friends, and the only humans who shared the Smith family's Wolfblood secret.

'Mmm,' Daniel answered thoughtfully. 'Well, I don't like the thing, and I don't like the way he's watching us.'

Daniel had no idea that his words were absolutely true – the owl was watching them, and so was Shannon.

Before giving Maddy her gift Shannon had carefully fitted a small movie camera behind one of the owl's eyes and linked it, wirelessly, to her laptop. It was now providing a wide-angle view of the den and Shannon could barely contain her excitement as she watched and waited for Maddy and her parents to transform.

She had made a camp in the woods close to the house and was huddled into a sleeping bag as she stared at the laptop, which was perched on a fallen tree.

Down from the heights of the moor the winter snow had melted away, although as night closed in the temperature was plummeting. But Shannon was so engrossed in watching the screen she hardly felt the cold, and she failed to hear the rustling in the nearby bushes.

'So there you are!'

Shannon spun around. 'Tom!' she said. 'You shouldn't creep up on people. How did you find me?'

'Your mum said you were staying over at Maddy's. So with it being full moon, I knew you couldn't be in the den with them, so I thought . . .' Tom paused as he noticed the moving images on Shannon's laptop. He stepped closer. 'Shannon, you haven't . . . you didn't . . .?'

'It's for *science*, Tom,' Shannon said hurriedly. 'It's vital that we learn all we can about Wolfbloods.'

'Maddy's not an experiment, Shan! She's our friend.'

Before discovering the truth about Maddy and her family three months earlier, Shannon had been convinced that some sort of wild beast was roaming the moor,

4

and had made it her mission to track it down. Now she was putting the same energy into learning all she could about Wolfbloods, even if it meant keeping some of her activities secret from Maddy.

'It's for science, Tom,' she repeated. She glanced at the laptop screen and her eyes widened. 'And look; look what's happening.'

Tom hesitated, knowing it was wrong to spy on Maddy and her parents, but almost as fascinated as Shannon to learn the mysteries of the Wolfblood den.

'They're transforming,' Shannon whispered.

Tom edged closer and saw for himself the way that Maddy and her parents dropped to all fours and swiftly changed from human form into wolves. But he immediately felt guilty for watching. 'You've got what you wanted, Shan, you've seen it happen. Now, let's go.'

'No, not yet, this is too important to miss. Just a little longer.'

They stared in awe, watching the wolves pad around the den, but then the smallest of the three became agitated, repeatedly jumping up at the old coal chute.

'It's Maddy,' Tom said, 'there's something wrong.'

'Yeah. Why is she behaving like that?'

'Maybe she wants to get out. Maybe she can smell us out here.'

'No, not from in there,' Shannon said, so fascinated by the behaviour of the three wolves that again she was oblivious to the sound of movement in the nearby bushes.

But Tom heard it. He turned to look. 'Shan . . .'

Completely absorbed in her task now, Shannon started using the voice recorder on her mobile to detail what she was seeing. 'Maddy is attempting to get out of the cellar,' she said into the microphone.

'Shan . . .' Tom said again.

'Her parents seem agitated too.'

'Shannon!' Tom said more loudly, and certain now that someone or something was approaching.

'Of course, this could be their natural reaction to being locked up.'

'*Shannon!*' Tom hissed.

'What?'

A low growl cut through the cold night air, and as Tom and Shannon stared a wolf emerged from the bushes. For a few seconds they were frozen with fear, but then they saw that the wolf looked completely exhausted and was in no condition to attack. It was panting heavily and could hardly lift its head to stare at them through baleful, yellow eyes.

'What do we do?' Tom whispered.

Shannon shook her head. Her eyes were fixed on the wolf. 'Rhydian?'

The wolf raised its head a little higher and stared at Shannon as if responding to the name.

'It is him!' Shannon said. 'It's Rhydian!'

Before Tom could answer a terrifying howl pierced the silence and was instantly answered by a second howl, and then a third.

'And he's brought friends,' Tom managed to gasp.

'They're not friends,' Shannon said. 'Run!'

Wolf-Rhydian somehow summoned the strength to run and Shannon and Tom sprinted after him, hurtling towards Maddy's house.

They reached the back yard, where wolf-Rhydian began scratching frantically at the shutters to the coal chute leading down to the den. But the shutters were held in place by a long metal pole pushed through the two handles. No wolf could move the pole – but Shannon could.

'I'll do it,' she screamed, as the howls of the chasing wolves grew louder and more terrifying.

She grabbed the pole and slid it free and then Tom yanked open one of the shutters.

'Go!' he yelled to wolf-Rhydian. 'Go!'

Wolf-Rhydian leapt into the darkness, and in the same moment, three ferocious, snarling and snapping wolves burst into the yard. They came to a halt as they saw Shannon and Tom standing by the hatch, but then began edging forward, yellow eyes glinting hungrily, vicious snarls emerging from deep in their throats.

Tom, still holding open one of the shutters, exchanged a look with Shannon. They both knew there was only one way to go. Shannon jumped into the coal chute and Tom immediately followed, the shutter slamming down as he plunged into darkness. He landed with a thud as the wolves outside howled their rage.

And then, much closer, Tom heard another deep, throaty growl.

Two

Back in human form, Daniel cautiously eased the back door open and sniffed the air as he peered outside. Daylight had brought a heavy, leaden sky, but there was no sight and little scent of the three intruder wolves.

Daniel stepped outside and was followed, equally cautiously, by Emma and Maddy. They, too, sniffed the air and slowly checked the yard, soon spotting the mass of paw prints around the shutters to the coal chute.

'I know Tom and Shannon didn't have a choice,' Emma said quietly to her daughter, 'but it was embarrassing for them to see us as wolves for the whole night. The den is private.'

Daniel was more concerned with the whereabouts of their unwanted visitors of the previous night. 'Not much scent; they didn't stay long.'

Rhydian, also back in human form, but pale and looking totally exhausted, lingered in the doorway. He was dressed in the same clothes he was wearing when they'd seen him last, three months earlier. But the clothes were ragged and dirty, his hair had grown long and was unwashed and there were scratches on his hands and neck. He looked a mess.

'The wild Wolfbloods hate the human world,' he muttered to Daniel. 'I didn't think they'd follow me this far.'

'And who exactly were they?' Emma asked. She looked angry.

'Alric, the pack leader, and two more, Aran and Meinir.'

'But why were they after you?' Maddy said. 'What happened?'

'I broke the rules.'

'What rules?' Emma demanded. 'Alpha wolves don't just leave their pack; you must have done something unforgivable. What was it?'

'Alric hated me, OK!' Rhydian snapped. 'Because I was new, and different from the rest of them, and I didn't obey all their stupid laws. In fact, he hated me for the same reasons you hate me.'

He turned away and went inside, Maddy and her parents following.

'Come on, Rhydian, we don't hate you,' Daniel said as he entered the kitchen, where Tom and Shannon hovered nervously by the cooker.

'You threw me out of your pack.'

'This isn't about us.' Emma was anxious to get the whole story. 'It's about why there's a wild alpha male roaming around our territory, putting us all in danger. And we didn't make you go; you chose to leave with your wild Wolfblood mother.'

Tom and Shannon looked embarrassed at having to listen to the argument.

'Er . . . excuse me,' Shannon said hesitantly, 'but Rhydian only left because Tom and me found out about you all being Wolfbloods.'

'And then you were going to leave too,' Tom added quickly. 'So what else could he do?'

Emma stared at them and then at Rhydian. 'But now he's in trouble and comes running back, we're supposed to welcome him with open arms, are we?'

'Yes, we are!' Maddy said angrily. 'We're his pack!'

Ever the peacemaker, Tom lifted a frying pan from the cooker and smiled. 'Breakfast, anyone?'

There was a long awkward silence but then Emma took the frying pan from Tom and everyone else shuffled to the table and sat down. Soon eggs and bacon were sizzling in the pan, but the mood in the kitchen remained tense and no one said a word.

When the food was ready Emma dished up a couple

of eggs and some rashers of bacon on to a plate. She hesitated for a moment, as if reaching a decision, before setting the plate down in front of Rhydian. He glanced up and nodded his thanks.

Maddy smiled, knowing that her mother had accepted Rhydian back into the pack, even if it was grudgingly. 'So how are we going to fix this?' she asked as her own breakfast arrived.

Emma and Daniel exchanged a look.

'We'll make some calls,' Daniel said. 'Social services, the Vaughans.'

Mr and Mrs Vaughan were the foster parents Rhydian had been living with up until running away.

'I can't see the Vaughans taking me back,' he said, spearing a piece of bacon. 'And you can't tell social services. They'd send me to a home!'

Daniel shook his head. 'There are people we can go to, Wolfbloods in positions of authority. They can solve problems the rest of us can't.'

Tom looked well impressed. 'Cool!' he said, nodding slowly. 'Like a . . . a sort of Wolfblood mafia.'

Shannon glared. 'Tom! Stop it!'

The hint of a smile crossed Emma's face for the first time that morning. 'But first we need to get you two home,' she said to Tom and Shannon. 'So that you can change for school.'

'Does that mean I'm staying at home for the day?' Maddy asked hopefully.

'No it does not,' her mother answered. 'Rhydian can stay here until we get things sorted, but you can go and get yourself ready. Now.'

Maddy, Tom and Shannon were dropped off at school a little later with strict instructions to say nothing about Rhydian until the new arrangements were sorted. Emma also warned them to remain on their guard, as the wild Wolfbloods might very well still be in the area.

Bradlington High School sat in the Northumbrian countryside, at one end of a wide valley, with panoramic views of woodlands, the moor and distant hills. If the wild Wolfbloods were still out there they had plenty of hiding places in which to lay low.

It was difficult for Maddy and her friends to concentrate on schoolwork. Maddy was worrying about Rhydian, while Tom had not forgiven Shannon for the toy owl trick and wanted her to remove the camera from the den at the earliest opportunity. But Shannon would not hear of it. She argued that when, one day, other people discovered Wolfbloods, the evidence she was gathering would help prove they could live peacefully among humans – some of them, at least.

The day passed slowly, with Maddy frequently checking her phone for a message from her mum, but by the end of the final lesson there was still no news. And there was to be no quick getaway from school.

The three friends were the leading, and often the only, members of the school's photography club and had agreed to take the photos at the first meeting of a brand new club that evening.

A school judo club was the idea of one of their form mates, Jimi Chen. Jimi took his sport very seriously; he was already a brown belt and reckoned to be pretty good for his age group.

He was proudly wearing his brown belt and judo suit as potential members of the new club filed into the gym. It was a mixed bunch; some with a genuine interest in taking part, others simply curious. Jimi's closest mates, Sam Dodds and Liam Hunter, were first to arrive. They were as surprised as everyone else when Kara, Katrina and Kay – famously known throughout the school as the Three Ks, swaggered in through the doors. The Ks were always together and were dedicated gatherers of gossip and followers of fashion. It was difficult to imagine any one of them risking smudging their make-up in a judo hold.

14

An instructor from Jimi's judo club was to lead the session, but the proud brown belt couldn't resist starting without him. 'In judo you never oppose strength with strength,' he told them all. 'Work out your opponent's attack and use their weaknesses against them.'

There were quite a few blank looks among the onlookers circled around Jimi, but Sam and Liam nodded thoughtfully, as though they knew exactly what the master was talking about.

'So,' Jimi asked, 'anyone want to try to put me on the ground?'

Kay's hand shot into the air. 'Me!'

Kara and Katrina stared. 'You!' they said together.

'I've always wanted to try judo,' Kay said, striding on to the mat and removing her enormous, circular earrings.

Jimi grinned. 'Brilliant.'

Without warning, Kay lunged forward, grabbing Jimi's judo suit with both hands, and for a split second it looked as though he might be barged over. But he swivelled and shifted his weight skilfully and the next moment Kay was flat out on the judo mat.

She sat up and stared at the fingers on one hand. 'He broke my nail!' she wailed.

'What?' Kara and Katrina shouted. They charged at Jimi and Kay leapt to her feet to join the battle, and soon it was Jimi's turn to find himself down on the mat. The gym was rocking with laughter.

'That's not fair,' Jimi complained as the three girls swapped high fives. 'Martial arts have strict rules, you can't just attack me.'

The door to the gym creaked open and the laughter stopped instantly.

'Rhydian Morris!' Katrina said, her eyes wide with surprise.

'Rhydian Morris!' Kara echoed.

'Where've you been?' Kay asked.

'Wow, you really need a haircut,' Kara added, as almost everyone in the gym clustered round to get a closer look at their former classmate.

Rhydian glanced towards Maddy but said nothing.

'Thought we'd seen the last of you,' Liam said.

'So where have you been, then?' Sam asked.

Rhydian still did not reply.

Katrina looked intrigued. 'Maybe he's been on the run.'

Kara was a lot more down to earth than her friend. 'What, from the hairdresser's?'

Jimi Chen and Rhydian had history, and not much of it good. 'When has running away made anyone a hero?' Jimi sneered as he got to his feet.

'No one called him a hero,' Maddy said quickly.

'No? So why's everyone crowding round him like he's some sort of rock star? He's just a kid who ran away.'

Rhydian smiled, remembering his previous battles with Jimi. They were nothing compared to what he'd been through over the past few months. 'What is this, then, Jimi?' he said, grinning at Jimi's outfit. 'A pyjama party?'

'Rhydian!' Maddy said quietly, attempting to calm the situation.

'It's judo, actually,' Jimi said, glaring at his old enemy.

Rhydian was in no mood to stay calm. 'Kids' stuff.'

Jimi took a deep breath. 'Really? Come on, then, put me down.'

The atmosphere in the gym was suddenly electric.

Jimi waited calmly as Rhydian slouched casually towards him, but then they grabbed each other and the battle was for real. Jimi was skilful, but Rhydian had hidden Wolfblood strengths, which he used to put his opponent on the floor.

'Amazing,' Katrina said, gazing at Rhydian.

Kara nodded. 'Yeah, well impressive.'

Even Tom and Shannon joined in the applause, but Maddy shook her head, knowing that this was not the way Rhydian should be returning to the school.

But he seemed content with his small victory over an old foe. He was walking away as Jimi sprang to his feet and with a furious yell went charging towards Rhydian.

Rhydian's Wolfblood instincts instantly engaged and Maddy saw his eyes flash yellow. He spun around and grasped the onrushing Jimi, and with one lightning movement and incredible strength, hurled him high into the air. Jimi crash-landed heavily on to a stack of judo mats.

Rhydian strode from the room without looking back as Sam and Liam rushed over to their friend.

'You all right, mate?' Liam asked anxiously.

Jimi sat up and nodded, winded but unhurt.

'Same old Rhydian,' Tom whispered to Maddy.

'No,' Maddy answered, shaking her head, 'I really don't think it is.'

The murmur of excited voices was echoing round the gym as the door swung open again and Mr Jeffries, their form teacher and head of year, strode in.

'How's it going, then?' he asked brightly. 'Has our expert arrived?' He spotted Jimi, who was still sitting on the mats. 'Ah, showing them how to fall, are you, Jimi? Very wise. Safety first – an excellent way to start.'

Three

Rhydian lingered in the school grounds, watching the judo club members leave, guessing that Maddy, Tom and Shannon would stay on to put away the photographic equipment. He could see that his return to the human world was not going to be easy. His three months with the wild Wolfblood pack had been totally different to everything he had known previously. Life was both a struggle for survival and a quest to stay secret, but there was also conflict within the pack, with rivals constantly juggling for position behind the leader.

Rhydian had been part of it all, and as his temper cooled, he quickly realised that his humiliation of Jimi was almost certainly a hangover from his time as a wild Wolfblood. And he already regretted what he'd done. He planned to go in to apologise to his three friends and then put things right with Jimi the following day, if he got the chance.

Suddenly, though, his Wolfblood senses were fully alert. He crouched, his eyes scanning the playing fields and the distant bushes as he sniffed the air and listened. Nothing, but they were there, he was certain they were there. He looked again and then saw them, Alric and the two other wild Wolfbloods, in human form, lurking in the bushes, waiting to strike.

Rhydian did not hesitate. He raced into the school building, knowing that before anything else, he had to try to get his friends to safety.

Maddy, Tom and Shannon were still in the gym, flicking through the judo photos on their camera screens.

'They're here!' Rhydian yelled as he burst through the door. 'Outside!'

Tom stared towards the door and then at Rhydian. 'You mean . . . those . . .?'

'Yes!' Rhydian said, turning to Maddy. 'Call your parents; get them here, and then you three stay inside. Alric won't come into school, not while there are humans in here. I'll go out and lead them away.'

'No, it's too dangerous,' Maddy gasped, 'you can't just go –'

'This is my fault!' Rhydian snapped. 'I brought them here.'

As Rhydian went to move away, Maddy grabbed his arm. 'All right, it's your fault, but you're not going out there alone!'

She looked at Tom and Shannon, who both nodded.

Rhydian hesitated, humbled that his friends were ready to stand by him as terrible danger threatened. 'But they're too strong for us.'

'I've got an idea,' Shannon said. 'Remember how Jimi told us that judo's about understanding your enemy and using their weaknesses against them?'

Tom didn't look convinced. 'I don't think judo's going to help here, Shan.'

'No, but Rhydian understands the wild pack. And we can use that.'

They looked towards Rhydian, who nodded.

Alric and his two underlings had crossed the open field and were huddled behind an outbuilding on the edge of the playground. Like all wild Wolfbloods they avoided human contact whenever possible to lessen the risk of discovery. And even being this close to buildings used by humans made them feel vulnerable and uncertain.

'We shouldn't be here,' Meinir moaned to the pack leader.

Aran was quick to agree. 'All this risk for one defiant cub. You've made your point. Alric, we should go.'

Alric was staring towards the double door they had seen Rhydian go through. 'We came for him, we don't leave without him!'

'But –'

Alric's head swung around and his eyes blazed. 'Are you challenging your leader?'

Aran slunk backwards, head lowered, fully aware that a challenge to the pack leader would be suicidal.

A creaking sound made the three wild Wolfbloods look over at the doors. Rhydian stood there.

Alric growled and began to stride towards Rhydian, with Meinir and Aran following hesitantly. But even Alric slowed as he got closer. It was almost unheard of for wild Wolfbloods to venture into a building.

'What's up, Alric?' Rhydian taunted. 'Scared of a few kids? Think they might bite?'

Alric's eyes went golden, the veins in his neck bulged and his blood turned silver. He was close to transforming as he snarled, 'Get him!'

Rhydian disappeared into the building as the three wild Wolfbloods raced across the playground. But at the entrance door they stopped, until Alric grabbed the others and shoved them inside. They stared down the long corridor. Rhydian glared back at them from the far end and as the Wolfbloods gave chase he went dashing away.

It was another desperate pursuit but this time, knowing the layout of the school, Rhydian had the advantage, and Shannon had given him an exact route to take. Along corridors, up one staircase and down another, darting around the main school building, Rhydian was just able to stay far enough in front of his pursuers.

And as the chase unfolded, Tom and Shannon darted from place to place – pressed against walls or in the wells of staircases – to take photo after photo of the three wild Wolfbloods. After a few frantic minutes they had captured all the evidence they needed. They ran to the gym, where Maddy had set up a projector and a large white screen.

'We got them!' Shannon yelled.

'This had better work!' Tom said as they gave the SD cards from their cameras to Maddy, who swiftly slotted them into the projector.

'Go!' she said, urgently to her friends. 'We can't let them smell you here.'

Tom and Shannon did not need telling twice. They rushed to the fire exit, crashed through the door and slammed it shut.

Seconds later, Rhydian arrived, skidding to a halt at Maddy's side as the three wild Wolfbloods burst into the room.

Alric grinned, confident now that he had Rhydian at his mercy. He sneered, his eyes lingering briefly on Maddy. 'Run to the tame wolf, have you, Rhydian? Well, she can't protect you.'

'Whatever Rhydian's done, it's over,' Maddy said bravely. 'You don't belong here.'

Alric glared and pointed a long bony finger at Rhydian. 'Tell that to him! He encouraged my pack to contaminate themselves with human contact!'

'It's not wrong to mix with humans!' Rhydian yelled.

'We mix with them and we become like them, we become weak,' Alric snarled. 'You brought weakness into my pack, and you'll pay for it!'

'And you're breaking the rules, now!' Maddy said. 'This is our territory, and Rhydian's one of our pack!'

Alric nodded. 'Brave words, but they will do you no good.'

He took a step forward and Maddy instantly pressed the start button on the remote control unit she was holding. As the wild Wolfbloods stared, images of them hurtling around the school began to scroll across the projector screen.

'Look at yourselves,' Maddy told them. 'The yellow eyes, the bulging veins. Look at the evidence we have.'

'Alric,' Meinir breathed anxiously.

'There are humans everywhere,' Aran continued. 'If they see this . . .'

'Yeah, what's the number one rule, Alric?' Rhydian shouted. 'Don't let the humans find out about us.'

Alric snarled and strode to the large screen, raised one hand and tore at the screen. But the pictures kept appearing, one after another, on the ripped material.

'They're still there,' Maddy continued courageously. 'They won't go away just because you rip the screen. And one click of a button and I can send the photos all around the world. Or . . .' She hesitated.

The wild Wolfbloods were far less assured as they turned from the screen to stare at Maddy.

'Or I can make this evidence disappear. If you leave now and never come back.'

'You have to do as the cub says,' Meinir said to Alric.

'We should never have entered human territory,' Aran added.

'Be quiet, you mewling cowards,' Alric growled. He glared at Maddy. 'Even a tame Wolfblood knows that the secret has to be kept.'

Maddy shook her head. 'The most important thing to me is my pack and my friends. If it means saving Rhydian, I'll tell the whole world.'

Alric hesitated, his eyes darting from Rhydian to Maddy. 'All right, we'll leave. You want Rhydian? You keep him. But remember this, your pack and my pack, we're enemies now.'

25

Without another word he stormed from the room, with Meinir and Aran scampering in his wake.

Maddy and Rhydian stood in stunned silence as the photos of the wild Wolfbloods continued to flicker across the ripped screen.

'Thanks,' Rhydian said eventually.

'It was Shannon's idea,' Maddy replied.

'Yeah, and I'll thank her, and Tom, as soon as we find them.' He glanced up at a photo of the snarling, golden-eyed Alric and then grinned. 'So, what was all that about telling the whole world to save Rhydian?'

Maddy felt herself blush. 'I had to say something. He wasn't going to just punish you, Rhydian, he was going to kill you.' She pressed the remote and the screen went blank.

Rhydian nodded. 'I'm glad I came back,' he said softly.

Maddy reddened even more. 'I'm glad too.'

Four

Wolfblood contacts in high places had been hard at work, speeding through the formalities and paperwork that authorised Daniel and Emma to become Rhydian's temporary foster parents.

Daniel and Emma had discussed the best way forward before hitting on what seemed the obvious and perfect solution. The house was large and rambling with plenty of spare rooms, and now that Emma had accepted Rhydian back as part of her pack, she wanted to do everything possible to make him feel at home, which included getting Daniel to frame some of his drawings.

Rhydian was a talented artist, a skill that had been forgotten while he was living wild. But not by Emma, who reckoned that going back to his art would help Rhydian's return to the human world. 'You don't have to hide your natural talents in this house, pet,' she told him as they looked at the framed drawings.

'We've been a bit hard on you,' Daniel added, 'so

this is just our way of saying welcome back to the pack.'

Emma checked her watch. 'And it's time for school. Where's Maddy?'

Maddy was running late. It was only when she cleared away the breakfast things she realised her clean school uniform was hanging on the washing line. Now she was hurrying to bring it in so that she could quickly run an iron over the trousers and blouse before dashing off with Rhydian to catch the school bus.

But as she stepped outside with the laundry basket clutched in both hands she suddenly stopped and sniffed the air. The scent was unmistakeable; it was another Wolfblood.

The girl was just a few metres away and was busy snatching Maddy's clothes from the washing line.

For a few seconds Maddy was too surprised to say anything, but then she yelled, 'Hey!'

The stranger spun around, her teeth bared, her eyes yellow and the veins in her neck already bulging and turning silver.

Maddy's own eyes blazed golden in response. 'Gimme my clothes!'

The girl went to make a dash for the woods, but Maddy moved swiftly to cut off her escape. She growled and snarled ferociously at Maddy, clutching her clothes to her chest.

She looked wild and untamed and, Maddy guessed, about her own age. But Maddy wasn't about to enter into a polite conversation; she wanted her clothes back, while the newcomer looked equally determined to hang on to them.

The veins in Maddy's neck turned silver as the two Wolfbloods moved towards each other, close to transforming and prepared to fight, just as Rhydian stepped out through the back door. 'Jana!'

Both girls wheeled around and Maddy could not miss the look of recognition that passed between Rhydian and the stranger. And there was something more than recognition, and whatever it was, it made Maddy even angrier.

Drawn by the shouting and snarling, Daniel and Emma appeared in the doorway. Seeing that she was heavily outnumbered, the girl Rhydian had called Jana went sprinting away, still holding Maddy's clothes.

Maddy went to give chase, but Rhydian grabbed her arm. 'No, Maddy!'

'Rhydian! She's got my clothes!'

'Let her go, she doesn't mean any harm.'

'How do you know? Who is she?'

Rhydian hesitated as Maddy, Daniel and Emma waited

for his reply. 'She's . . . she's Jana. Alric's daughter.'

Maddy glared furiously while Daniel rolled his eyes and Emma sighed. 'Here we go again,' she muttered.

'She's got half my wardrobe,' Maddy snapped. 'And if you lot hadn't scared her away I'd have got it back.'

Emma was staring at Rhydian. 'Why is she here? Why did she come to the one house where she might be recognised?'

'Alric can't know she's here.' Rhydian seemed as puzzled as the Smith family. 'He wouldn't put Jana in danger; she's everything to him. There's no way he'd allow her to come and steal a few clothes. I could try to find her; see what's going on.'

'No,' Daniel said firmly. 'If the pack have come back, you might be lured into a trap.'

Maddy was still seething. 'Then what do we do?'

'You go to school as normal,' her mum said. 'We'll think of something.'

But the school day was to be anything but normal.

Rhydian had made a fragile peace with Jimi after the gymnasium judo incident, but the hostility between them still festered.

Before morning registration Jimi and his mates, Liam and Sam, had met up by their lockers, where Jimi was

30

explaining how a delivery of meat had been stolen from his dad's hotel the previous day.

'What, all they took was meat?' Liam asked.

Jimi nodded. 'The butcher had just delivered it. The chef turned his back for a moment and when he looked round some girl was running off with it.'

Rhydian and Maddy, with Tom and Shannon, were also making their way to the lockers to gather the bits and pieces they would need during the morning. It seemed like the beginning of a perfectly normal day, but then everything changed. As Rhydian looked up and glanced down the long corridor he saw students standing back against the walls as a girl strode confidently through their midst.

It was Jana. Grubby and unwashed, her hair a tangled mess, and dressed in Maddy's school uniform.

'Oh no,' Rhydian groaned.

Shannon stared. 'She's wearing your –'

'I know!' Maddy hissed.

Rhydian ran to Jana. 'What are you doing here?'

'Going to school, just like you do. Like a human.'

'But you can't be here!'

'Why not? You were the one who said I should try living like a human.'

'But that was when . . .' Rhydian clammed up as he saw Jimi and his mates approaching.

Jimi sneered when he spotted Rhydian and then exaggeratedly clutched at his throat as though he could hardly breathe. 'What's going on, Welshie?' he gasped. 'Have you started some sort of charity called Stinkoes R Us? Your new girlfriend reeks!'

There was no disguising the fact that Jana certainly did smell, and Sam and Liam added to the joke by pinching their noses and grimacing.

Jana did not understand exactly what Jimi was talking about but she knew enough to realise he was making fun of her. And she didn't like it one bit. Rhydian saw her eyes blaze golden and the veins in her neck begin to bulge. Before anyone else noticed the change, he grabbed the wild Wolfblood, pushed her along the corridor past Maddy, Tom and Shannon and bundled her into the photographic darkroom.

'So now what do we do?' Tom said, gazing at the closed door.

'Dunno,' Shannon said.

'You go to registration,' Maddy told them both. 'I'll help Rhydian sort this.'

'No way,' Tom said. 'Not if she's a danger to you.'

'It's not me,' Maddy breathed, 'she's a danger to you. She's a wild Wolfblood and wild Wolfbloods have killed people who discovered their secret. If she finds out that you know . . .'

'We're on our way,' Tom said, pulling Shannon with him towards their registration classroom.

Maddy went into the darkroom, where Rhydian stood guard over Jana, who had managed to control her temper. But her eyes flashed yellow again at the sight of Maddy.

'You stole my clothes,' Maddy said before Jana had the chance to speak. 'And now you walk into school like you belong here.'

'I do what I want,' Jana sneered. 'And I don't answer to tame Wolfbloods.'

For a moment it looked as though the two Wolfbloods were about to resume where they'd left off earlier that morning, but Rhydian quickly stepped between them.

'Yeah, all right, all right!' He turned to Maddy. 'Look, let's hear what she's got to say, eh?'

Maddy took a deep breath, bringing her wolf instincts under control. She nodded.

'Why are you here?' Rhydian asked Jana. 'Did Alric send you after me?'

All Jana's bluster and confidence suddenly disappeared. 'He threw me out! I just wanted to see what human life was like and he called me a traitor!' She went to Rhydian, threw her arms around his neck and buried her face in his chest. 'I don't know anyone outside my pack,' she sobbed. 'Only you. Please let me stay.'

Rhydian was looking over Jana's head at Maddy, who was struggling to contain her anger.

'Of course you can stay,' Rhydian said eventually.

'What?' Maddy was fuming.

'Look, Maddy, when your parents didn't want me around, you told them they had a duty to help me. Well, now we have a duty to help Jana.'

'But it's not as simple as that. You can't just walk her into class.'

'Can't I?' Rhydian considered this for a moment. 'Just watch me.'

He opened the door and as Maddy saw Jana being marched away she couldn't fail to notice the way the wild Wolfblood glanced back at her with a look of triumph in her eyes.

Five

Mr Jeffries didn't exactly take Jana's arrival in his stride. He liked everything in order and order in everything, and was bewildered by the arrival of a new pupil without all the relevant and necessary paperwork. But Rhydian managed to convince his form teacher that Jana was from a family of travellers and that her paperwork might just have been delayed.

So the new girl was allowed to stay while enquiries were made. She took a seat next to Rhydian, which infuriated Maddy even more when she walked into class a little later, especially as she had been on the phone to her parents asking for their help with the new situation.

Jana was the centre of attention, particularly with the Three Ks, who were both intrigued by the new girl and highly offended by the strong aroma that wafted around her.

'Smells like manure,' Kay whispered to her friends.

'Absolutely stinks,' Kara added.

'It is disgusting,' Katrina confirmed.

Jana's heightened Wolfblood hearing meant she could hear every whispered word.

'Calm down,' Rhydian muttered as he spotted the veins in the back of her hands start to darken. 'You have to ignore them.'

Somehow, they made it through to morning break, when Maddy took Rhydian and Jana aside, having reminded Tom and Shannon to keep their distance. 'Mum's not happy,' she whispered to Rhydian.

'Why am I not surprised?'

'But she's talking to the people who sorted out social services for you.' She turned to Jana. 'They can create a history for you, but it'll take time.'

Jana smiled ingratiatingly. 'Thank you. You're really clever.'

Maddy wasn't sure whether or not she believed either the smile or the thanks but she told herself that it didn't really matter. What mattered was keeping the Wolfblood secret. 'You need to try to fit in and keep your head down,' she said to Jana. 'And you can't show your wolf side, *ever*.'

'I know. I won't.'

'And . . .'

'What?' Jana said.

'You *really* need a shower.'

Jana looked at Rhydian. 'Do I?'

Rhydian nodded. 'Oh yes.'

'Come on,' Maddy said with a sigh. 'I'll take you.'

By lunchtime, Maddy was beginning to think that they might just make it through the day without disaster striking.

There had been a close call during a drama lesson with Miss Fitzgerald when Jana came close to wolfing out after she was asked to improvise a scene with The Ks. The action turned nasty and Jana looked to be turning wolf, but Maddy and Rhydian leapt in to drag her away. And they were so good at making Miss Fitzgerald believe that their intervention was all part of the improvisation that she complimented them on their acting skills.

Maddy was tentatively leading Jana into the dining hall and explaining for at least the tenth time why it would not be OK to ask for raw meat when Tom and Shannon suddenly joined them. Both smiled broadly at Jana.

'Hi, Jana,' Tom said, brightly. 'We've not been properly introduced, but I'm Tom, Maddy's mate. And this is Shannon.'

Shannon was equally welcoming. 'Hello, Jana, it's great to have you here.'

'Is it?' Jana said, looking puzzled.

'Oh, yeah, really great,' Tom said. 'Come on, let's get some lunch.'

Before Maddy could intervene, Tom had hurried Jana away.

'What's going on?' Maddy said quietly to Shannon. 'You know it's dangerous.'

'Yeah, well, Tom and me decided that if you want her to fit in, we have to act normally.'

'But I don't want her to fit in,' Maddy found herself confessing. 'I want her to go back to the wild where she belongs.'

Shannon raised her eyebrows. 'And stop getting between you and Rhydian?'

'This isn't about Rhydian.'

Shannon didn't look convinced.

They joined Tom and Jana in the queue for lunch, and as she stood waiting, Maddy saw the Three Ks walk over to Jimi Chen and his mates at a nearby table. And from the looks they were giving Jana, it appeared that the Ks had mischief in mind.

'Hey, Jimi,' Katrina said loudly, 'I heard some meat got nicked from your dad's hotel.'

Jimi looked mystified. 'So?'

Kara turned deliberately towards Jana. 'By some wild-looking girl?'

'Bit of a coincidence, that, eh, Jimi?' Kay added. 'Your meat gets nicked and *she* turns up the next day.'

Jimi finally saw what they were getting at. He got to his feet and strode over to Jana and Tom, who by now, both had trays of food.

'Were you on the rob last night?' Jimi said, glaring at Jana.

Sensing a problem, Tom did his best to diffuse the situation. 'Jimi, what are you talking about?'

'I'm talking to her,' Jimi said, his eyes fixed on Jana's. 'Someone stole meat from our hotel last night, and my money's on you.'

Jana laughed. 'Why would I want your stinky meat? I bet it smells as bad as you do.'

She went to walk on but Jimi grabbed one arm. Moving like lightning, Jana snatched her lunch plate from the tray and pushed it into his face. The dining hall erupted with laughter as Jimi stood frozen with gravy running down his cheeks and bits of potato stuck to his chin. But Jimi was a fighter too. Calmly, he lifted a dish of fruit and custard from the tray and tipped it over Jana's head.

The room was in uproar as Rhydian arrived in the doorway. 'Oh no,' he gasped, as he saw the food-splattered Jana and Jimi leap at each other and go crashing on to the floor. They rolled under a table, locked in ferocious battle.

Maddy was already hurtling into action as the chant of, 'Fight, fight, fight!' echoed around the room. Knowing she had to drag Jana away before she transformed, Maddy threw herself on to the floor and grabbed one of the wild Wolfblood's legs.

'Stop that at once!' Miss Fitzgerald's voice boomed around the room. 'I said *stop*!'

The dining hall went silent and the battle beneath the table ceased. Slowly Jimi and Jana crawled into view, with Maddy, Rhydian, Tom and Shannon all fearing the worst. But apart from a face plastered with custard and fruit, Jana looked completely human. Somehow she had stopped herself from wolfing out and disaster had been averted once more.

Maddy and Rhydian were waiting outside the head-master's office when Jana and Jimi emerged.

Jimi just scowled at them both and stormed away but Jana stopped and shrugged her shoulders. 'The head-master said he was giving me a detention but then he didn't give me anything.'

Rhydian laughed. 'I've got a feeling you'll learn all about detentions if you manage to stay here for much longer.'

'*If*,' Maddy added doubtfully.

As they went to walk away, Mr Jeffries came hurrying up. 'Ah, there you are, Jana. I've just been on to the Education Authority.'

Maddy and Rhydian exchanged a look, fearing that the deception had been uncovered.

'They sent your paperwork to the wrong school,' Mr Jeffries continued. 'They're sending it all over to us now.'

Jana's eyes widened. 'So . . . that means . . .?'

'Yes, welcome to Bradlington High. Just try not to get into too many food fights in future, eh?'

Six

Daniel's usually sunny face was dark with worry. 'She has to go, by the end of the week and preferably before. Wild Wolfbloods don't belong in the human world.'

'But she's really trying, Dad,' Maddy said.

'You heard your father.' Emma looked as concerned and worried as her husband. 'There's no way she can stay in Stoneybridge.'

They were back at the house, where Maddy and Rhydian had just detailed the events of their school day.

'You can't force her to leave,' Rhydian said.

'We called in a lot of favours to get the paperwork arranged so quickly,' Daniel answered. 'But it's too much of a risk to let her stay around. Travellers move on all the time. When she goes, we'll just let it be known that her family have moved on.'

'Where is she?' Emma was holding the keys to the Land Rover.

Maddy hesitated before replying. 'There's an abandoned caravan near Benson's Farm.'

'Right, you two stay here.'

Before Maddy and Rhydian could argue further, Daniel and Emma had gone. Seconds later the Land Rover coughed into life and went trundling away down the track.

Maddy and Rhydian sat in a thoughtful silence for a few minutes. 'This is our pack's territory,' Maddy said eventually. 'Mum and Dad just don't want her here.'

'Why does it always have to be about packs? Doesn't Jana get a choice? Come on, Maddy, she's one of us.'

The abandoned caravan Jana had chosen to make her home was rusty and leaky and rested precariously on two punctured tyres. But it was more than Jana was accustomed to in the wild. She was holding one of Maddy's blouses and admiring her reflection in a cracked mirror when she heard the Land Rover pull up.

Jana was outside even before Emma and Daniel emerged from the vehicle. The three Wolfbloods eyed each other warily.

'Is this about the clothes?' Jana asked.

'It's about you,' Daniel said. 'We want you gone.'

'But I can't leave. I don't know anyone but my pack. And my father says I'm a traitor.'

Emma was not going to be swayed. 'Pack up and leave. Tonight.'

'And if I don't?' Jana had switched instantly from being passive and defensive to aggressive and ready to attack. Her eyes flashed yellow and the veins in the back of her hands and her neck began to bulge and darken.

But Emma was not going to be cowed by a young Wolfblood, however brave. She began veining, too, and it looked as though a fight was about to start when Maddy and Rhydian burst into the clearing. They had run at Wolfblood speed to get there.

'You can't drive her away, Mam,' Maddy yelled. 'She won't survive on her own.'

'There's no room for any more strays in our pack.' Emma had controlled her wolf side but was still fixing Jana with a hostile stare. 'Especially not Alric's daughter.'

'But she doesn't have to be in our pack! She can look after herself. Here!'

'Maddy, she's just a kid,' Emma said.

'Who lives in the wild! She's used to looking after herself.'

'Maddy, she *is* wild,' Daniel snapped. 'She'll be discovered.'

'No, we can help her, Rhydian and me.'

Rhydian had remained silent but he nodded his agreement as Emma and Daniel looked at him. Emma, though, was still far from convinced. 'How can you two help when she wolfs out in front of your class-mates?'

'But I won't wolf out!' Jana sensed a glimmer of hope. 'I can control my wolf side, I did it today.'

'She did, Mam,' Maddy added quickly. 'She can do it, she can fit in!'

Emma hesitated. 'And where would she live?'

'Here!' Jana said.

'That's ridiculous!'

'To us, yes,' Rhydian said. 'But not to a wild Wolfblood.'

The night air was bitterly cold and a frost was begin-ning to appear on the ground.

'A week in that rusty old thing and she'll be fleeing back to the wild,' Daniel said to Emma. 'In the meantime, if the kids think they can handle it, maybe we should let them try.'

Emma was wavering. 'All right,' she said at last to Jana. 'But one whiff of trouble and you'll be out of our territory quicker than you can bay at the moon. Understand?'

Jana nodded slowly.

Back at the house Maddy was watching Rhydian hang the last of his framed drawings on the bedroom wall.

'Thanks for backing up Jana,' he said, standing back to look at the drawing.

'She's one of us, what else was I meant to do? I hope she's OK in that old caravan.'

Rhydian turned to face Maddy. 'Look, I should have told you about her and I should have told her about you.'

'Yeah,' Maddy answered. 'You should.'

'Out there in the wild,' Rhydian said, crossing to the window, 'some bits were great: my mum, and my brother, Bryn. But some stuff was strange and a bit scary. Jana helped me survive. She was the only one I could trust.'

Outside, hidden in the shadows and cloaked by the dark night, Jana had engaged her Wolfblood hearing to listen to every word of their conversation.

She smiled and then crept noiselessly away.

Seven

Liam Hunter had big news, and for once it meant he was firmly in the spotlight rather than in his usual role as one of Jimi Chen's loyal followers. And Jimi didn't mind one bit, because the hot news was that Liam's dad, a farmer, had unearthed a skeleton while ploughing a field.

A crowd had gathered at school to study the photographs Liam had taken on his phone and to listen to his excited description of the discovery. 'The skull's not normal; there's something totally different about it. And my dad was telling me that an ancestor of ours was a werewolf hunter.'

'Hunter by name, werewolf hunter by profession,' Jimi said, grinning.

Liam beamed, revelling in being the centre of attention.

The Three Ks looked suitably and scarily impressed, while others seemed more sceptical. Tom and Shannon exchanged a troubled look, knowing that while werewolves were unlikely, to say the least, there had

47

definitely been Wolfbloods in the area for many hundreds of years.

Maddy, Rhydian and Jana arrived and heard the word 'werewolf' rippling through the assembled crowd.

'So my dad's called in a scientist to examine it,' Liam continued.

'Examine what?' Rhydian asked. 'What's going on?'

'Look at this,' Liam said, thrusting his phone towards Rhydian. 'My dad ploughed up a werewolf skeleton this morning, that's the skull. And *my* ancestor killed it!'

Jana's eyes blazed, and Maddy could see that she was ready to fly at Liam as he boasted of the killing. She grabbed Jana's arm. 'Calm down,' she whispered.

'*Calwearas* are all the same,' Jana sneered as Liam and his friends went swaggering away.

'Don't call them that,' Rhydian said, noticing Maddy's confused look. 'It means "baldies",' he told her. 'It's what wild Wolfbloods call all humans.'

Maddy shook her head. 'Charming.'

'People like him almost wiped us out!' Jana said. 'And if that is a Wolfblood skeleton . . .'

'Yeah, we need to know,' Maddy said, interrupting. 'But we have to be careful. We'll go up to the field at break time and take a look.'

'Why don't we go now?'

'We can't now. We're at school, we can't just miss lessons, even if we want to.'

'School!' Jana hissed and went storming away. She did not look happy.

'I'll keep an eye on her,' Rhydian said to Maddy before hurrying after the wild Wolfblood.

Tom and Shannon had been waiting for the opportunity of a private word with Maddy.

'Are you going to check it out?' Shannon asked eagerly as they joined her.

Maddy nodded. 'At break time.'

'Great, we'll meet you in the playground.'

'No, Shan, you can't come! Neither of you can come.'

'But why?'

'Jana's going to be there and you're not supposed to know about us, remember?'

The skeleton was big and the skull clearly appeared to be more wolf than human. Jana sank to the ground to touch the bones and then closed her eyes.

'What's she doing?' Maddy asked Rhydian.

'It's called Ansion. Some wild Wolfbloods can do it, not many. It's supposed to connect you to nature in an even deeper way than Eolas, like I showed you before. It lets you . . . know things.'

Jana was breathing deeply and rhythmically. Suddenly her eyes snapped open; they were a vivid yellow. 'He was killed during transformation!'

'You can see that?' Maddy asked.

Jana nodded. 'It's hard to explain.' She stared up at Maddy. 'And . . .'

'What?'

'He was a member of your pack!'

'No, he couldn't be. I'd know if someone in my family had been killed.'

'It was a long time ago. We have to bury him properly.'

She began scrabbling at the ground, digging around the skeleton to lift it from the earth. But as Maddy went to join her, they heard the sound of engines and looked up to see two heavy vehicles turning into the field from the road.

'We mustn't be seen,' Maddy said quickly as Jana continued to claw at the earth.

The vehicles stopped and a woman got out and peered across the field towards them.

Rhydian managed to pull Jana to her feet and they started to run towards the treeline.

'Hey!' the woman called.

Maddy stopped and glanced back and for a moment locked eyes with the distant woman. Then she turned and ran on.

A series of phone calls over the lunch break sparked a flurry of urgent activity. Maddy spoke to her parents to tell them about the suspected Wolfblood skeleton. Daniel said that as the family had been in the area for over four hundred years it was quite possible that it was a relative. He was going to head off to the local records office to discover what he could. Emma, ever cautious, warned Maddy, Rhydian and Jana to keep well clear of the skeleton and the proposed scientific exploration.

But that proved to be impossible, as Mr Jeffries had also been busy on the phone. An old colleague from his university days was in charge of the dig and had agreed that Mr Jeffries' class could come and observe the removal of the skeleton that afternoon.

By the time they trooped on to the site the area had changed dramatically. A large and well-equipped forensic tent had been erected over the shallow grave and the skeleton was already fully exposed, although still lying in the earth.

The students gazed in awe as they filed past and gathered round. Maddy felt strange that the bones could be those of a long-dead relative, and Jana was clearly agitated that a crowd had been allowed to gawp disrespectfully at a long-dead Wolfblood.

And it was clear to everyone now that the bones did not look like those of a normal human being.

'So, I'm a forensic scientist,' Dr Rebecca Whitewood told them. Maddy recognised her as the woman who had spotted her running from the site earlier. 'I presume you know what a forensic scientist does.'

Shannon was quick to answer. 'You use scientific methods to look for evidence and link suspects to the scene of a crime.'

'Very good,' Dr Whitewood said.

'So are the police involved in this?' Maddy asked anxiously.

'No, not this time,' Dr Whitewood said, after a moment. 'I have a personal interest in skeletons, and I can tell you that this one is approximately two hundred years old.'

Jana nudged Maddy. 'Told you.'

'And it's unique,' Dr Whitewood added.

Liam couldn't resist butting in. 'Yeah, because it's a werewolf.'

There were far fewer sceptical looks than when Liam had first come up with the word 'werewolf' earlier in the day, and even Dr Whitewood raised her eyebrows as if to suggest the idea wasn't a complete impossibility.

A few months earlier, Shannon would have been thrilled at the mention of a werewolf, but now she had her Wolfblood friends to protect. 'Oh, come on,' she said dismissively, 'of all the possible explanations that's the least likely. It's much more plausible that it's a human with some kind of genetic mutation, or a hoax – Victorian freak shows were full of them. You know, animal bones mixed in with human ones and billed as some kind of monster.'

Dr Whitewood was clearly impressed. 'You've obviously done your research. And you are?'

'Shannon. Shannon Kelly.'

'Well, you're right to err on the side of caution, Shannon, but I wonder what you'd make of something we found just before you arrived?'

She gestured to her assistant, who took a clear plastic container from a larger case. Inside the container was a small metal ball, which he handed to Dr Whitewood.

'What is it?' Shannon asked.

'It's a musket ball; we removed it from the skeleton. And very curiously, it's made of silver.'

Liam's eyes lit up. 'And silver bullets kill werewolves! I told you!'

Dr Whitewood smiled. 'It certainly suggests that whoever shot this . . . creature . . . may have thought it was such a beast, but fortunately we don't have to rely on speculation. Once we're back in the lab I'll be running DNA tests to discover exactly what these bones are.'

Eight

A DNA test meant terrible danger. Maddy and Rhydian knew that only too well from the time that samples of their blood had been analysed. And now it looked as though the DNA of two-hundred-years-old bones would finally reveal the Wolfblood secret to the world. Somehow they had to stop the test from happening.

And there was an added problem; Jana was insisting they snatch the skeleton away from the scientists in order to give the long-dead Wolfblood a proper burial.

'We have to do it,' she told them. 'When a Wolfblood dies, the living must guide his soul to the One Pack in the afterlife. Without that he's lost for eternity.'

Maddy didn't agree with Jana on many things but she had to admit that it wasn't right for the Wolfblood to have been buried in a field with no real ceremony.

As class broke up for the day, she called Rhydian and Jana aside. 'You two go and fetch a shovel and a spade, and I'll hang on here.'

'And where are we meant to get a shovel and a spade from?' Rhydian asked.

'From the shed at our place. It's not locked.'

'But that's miles away.'

Maddy didn't have time to argue. 'And you're Wolfbloods. You can be there and back in a few minutes if you get going now.'

They got going, hurtling away at incredible speed, faster than any human would have believed possible if they'd spotted them.

Next Maddy asked Shannon and Tom to loiter around the forensic tent and delay Dr Whitewood's departure from the site for as long as possible.

Then she put in another call to her parents. Emma and Daniel had just emerged from the records office, where they had learned that the Wolfblood probably was a relative. 'It looks as though it's your great-great-great-great-uncle William,' Daniel said. 'He disappeared about two hundred years ago and there's no death recorded for him.'

'So Jana was right,' Maddy said.

'We can't be absolutely certain, but then neither can that scientist.'

'That's where you're wrong, Dad. She's got a thing

about werewolves and she's determined to get to the truth by analysing the skeleton's DNA.'

'What? We can't let her do that. We'll drive over,' Daniel said.

'No, it'll take too long. I have to do something now!'

She ended the call but her mobile immediately started ringing. It was Shannon, calling from inside the forensic tent.

'Shan, what's happening?'

'They've packed the bones into two blue boxes,' Shannon whispered. 'They'll be loading them into the vehicles any minute and then they're going back to the university. I don't know what more I can do, Mads.'

'Just keep them talking for a bit longer.'

'Talking about what? I've said everything I know about skeletons and bones, I even made a terrible joke about spare ribs, which did not impress her. I can see she suspects something's going on and she's certain she saw you hanging about here this morning.'

'Just a bit longer, Shan, I know you can do it.'

A few minutes later Dr Whitewood's assistant emerged from the tent with the two blue boxes Shannon had mentioned. He put them into the back of one of the vehicles and returned to the tent just as Rhydian and Jana arrived, carrying the spade and the shovel.

'What kept you?' Maddy asked.

Rhydian was not amused. 'Very funny. What now?'

Maddy gestured towards the vehicle. 'The bones are in there. Doctor Whitewood and the assistant are in the tent with Tom and Shannon. We have to make sure they stay in the tent while we get the bones.'

Rhydian looked at the tent and smiled; no further explanation was necessary. 'Nice one.'

All three young Wolfbloods went tearing towards the tent and in seconds had wrenched from the ground or kicked away the guy ropes holding up the canvas.

The tent collapsed and beneath the heavy canvas, Dr Whitewood and the others yelled and struggled to get free. But Maddy and Jana leapt from place to place on the canvas, treading it down, to ensure there would be no quick and easy escape.

By the time a bedraggled Dr Whitewood emerged into daylight there was no one to be seen. And the boxes and the bones had disappeared.

Maddy, Rhydian and Jana were deep in the woods, staring down at the bones in the two blue boxes.

Jana looked particularly thoughtful. 'Tom and

Shannon,' she said at last, 'what will you tell them about the bones?'

Maddy took a deep breath. 'The truth.'

'Maddy, don't,' Rhydian said. 'If you tell . . .'

'No, Rhydian, I'm not lying any more, it only makes things worse.' She turned to Jana. 'Tom and Shannon helped us get the skeleton bones because they know about us.'

Jana looked ready to explode. 'They know who we are?'

'Yes, they know! Because I told them.'

'You told *calwearas*! You broke the oath!'

'I didn't take an oath!' Maddy yelled. 'That's your pack; you do oaths. Tom and Shannon are part of my pack and we don't!'

'They can't be in a pack! *Calwearas* can't be trusted!'

'Look, Jana,' Rhydian said, trying to calm the situation, 'they're our friends. And they helped us get the bones, which is what you wanted. And they can be trusted; *we* trust them.'

'And we care about them,' Maddy added. 'So if you stay around, you're going to have to learn to trust them too.'

The burial ceremony took place later that evening. They decided to return old Uncle William's bones to Smith land and Daniel had chosen a suitable spot in the ancient woodland.

'I think he'd like it here,' he said to Emma as they watched Jana scatter herbs and mutter the last few words of the burial ritual.

'May these bones be blessed, Oh, Friogearde. Guide this spirit to the One Pack, where we hunt proudly for eternity.'

Maddy and Rhydian stood watching, next to Emma and Daniel. Tom and Shannon had been invited to join them for the ceremony but were keeping a respectful distance.

'We're almost done,' Jana said. 'All that's left is the final blessing.'

The five Wolfbloods joined hands but then Jana turned to Tom and Shannon, holding one hand towards them. 'Tom . . . Shannon . . .?'

Shannon's eyes widened. 'Us?'

Jana nodded.

'Really?' Tom said.

She nodded again and the five became seven as they formed a circle around the grave.

Maddy and her parents, Rhydian and Jana looked up at the starry sky and then opened their mouths and howled. As the sound echoed away into the night, Tom and Shannon looked at each other. Tom shrugged his shoulders and then they both threw back their heads and howled too.

Nine

The morning was cold and bright, and Jana was perfectly content as she stepped from the caravan she had made home and strode off into the woodland. The ancient van was run-down and dilapidated, but to a Wolfblood accustomed to living rough in the wild, it was the height of luxury.

Jana had come to know the surrounding woodland extremely well. She moved quickly and effortlessly along narrow tracks, through dips and hollows and over tiny streams as she took the quickest way towards school.

Suddenly she stopped and sniffed the air, sensing that she was being watched. There was no sound, nothing moved, but Jana's heightened Wolfblood senses made her certain that she was not alone in the heart of the woodland.

She moved on, treading lightly, listening and watching, ready to respond to any threat. But even Jana was not quick enough as, seemingly out of nowhere and at lightning speed, her father, Alric, loomed into view and was standing in front of her.

Jana staggered back as her father's piercing and terrifying eyes met hers. And then Alric grinned and held his arms wide open. 'Jana!'

With a giggle of delight, Jana ran into her father's arms and they hugged each other tightly.

'I've missed you so much,' Alric breathed.

'And I've missed you, Dad.'

They sat together on a fallen log and Alric studied his daughter's face for long moments. 'We expected you back by now.'

'The job's been harder than I thought,' Jana said.

'That's not good.'

'It takes time, Dad, I'm working on him.'

'But there is no more time, Jana.'

'What do you mean?'

'The pack is getting restless; questioning my authority.' Alric looked worried. 'They won't wait any longer. If Rhydian is to be forgiven he needs to return now.'

'But he's made a home here; he won't give it up easily.'

Alric's temper suddenly flared. 'His home is the pack and your job is to bring him back, that was always the plan.' He paused for a moment and then spoke more gently. 'No one should lose their roots. The three of us will return to the wilderness, tonight.'

'*Tonight!*'

Alric nodded. 'Rhydian's time in the human world is finished. You have to make him see this.'

Jana's mind was in turmoil by the time she arrived at school. Her father's ultimatum meant that it was not just Rhydian's time in the human world that was about to come to an end – it was hers too. And that worried her far more than she had imagined it might.

It had always been her mission to bring Rhydian back to the wilderness, but she had not expected the mission to be over so soon. And she had no choice in the matter – her father was the pack leader and his orders had to be obeyed.

There was no chance to speak quietly to Rhydian during the first couple of lessons, but at break time she cornered him in the playground, having spent the last hour trying to work out the best way of broaching the subject. 'I . . . I had a dream last night. About the wilderness and our pack.'

Rhydian nodded but didn't look particularly interested. His thoughts were firmly in the human world.

'Don't you miss the wild, Rhydian?'

Rhydian shrugged. 'Not really.'

'No timetables? No school?'

'It's not so bad here.'

Jana sighed; she was making little progress. 'But sometimes you must think about returning to the wild? All the freedom?'

'There wasn't much freedom for me, Jana,' Rhydian said. 'And your dad tried to kill me.'

'But what if he forgave you and gave you a second chance?'

'Alric's not the forgiving type. And he threw you out, remember?'

'He'll forgive me; I know he will. And you, too.'

Rhydian did not reply.

Jana raised one hand and gently placed it on Rhydian's chest. 'Don't you feel the call of the wild in your heart? It's where your family is; your blood.'

'No.' Rhydian's reply was emphatic. 'Everything that's important to me is here now.'

Jana sighed. Her opening tactics had failed miserably.

Maddy was on the other side of the playground with Tom and Shannon. She had spotted Rhydian and Jana and was about to join them when she realised that they were having what looked like a very earnest conversation. Maddy couldn't stop herself from wanting to know what was being said.

Tom and Shannon were in the midst of their own discussion about the lesson that had just finished, so it was simple enough for Maddy to engage her Wolfblood hearing to eavesdrop on what was being said on the far side of the playground.

'All right, I'll tell you the truth,' she heard Jana say to Rhydian.

'The truth? What d'you mean?' Rhydian replied.

'But you must promise not to tell Maddy, or anyone.'

Maddy felt herself blush, but it didn't stop her from listening.

'Why?'

'Just promise!'

'All right, I promise.'

Maddy looked away as she saw Jana glance quickly in her direction. Tom and Shannon chatted on, but Maddy was totally focused on what Jana and Rhydian were saying.

'My father turned up this morning,' she heard Jana say very softly.

'What?'

'He's in the woods. And he's come to make peace.'

'No,' Rhydian said. 'No, I don't believe it.'

'He knows he went too far, but he's made an offer.'

'What sort of offer?'

'He says if you and I return to the pack and swear allegiance to him, then we can live in peace again.'

'No way! No, I'm not going back, end of story.'

On the far side of the playground, Maddy was suddenly aware that Tom and Shannon were both staring at her.

'Sorry? What did you say?'

'You weren't listening at all, were you, Mads?' Tom said.

'Yes! I was.'

'So what exactly were we talking about?'

'You were saying . . . er. . . I . . .' It was no use; she had to confess. 'I'm sorry, I was thinking about something else.'

The bell for the end of break sounded and everyone in the playground began to head for their next classroom. By the time Maddy had re-engaged her Wolfblood hearing, Rhydian and Jana were on the move and their conversation was blurred by the voices of others around them. But Maddy clearly heard Jana say, 'I don't have a choice, so unless you come with me I'll never see you again.'

Jana returned to the woods at lunchtime and found her father waiting impatiently. And there was no mistaking the look of disappointment in Alric's eyes when his daughter told him that Rhydian had refused to even consider his offer. But there was more, something Jana had never previously seen in her father – fear.

'Then I can't be held responsible.' His voice was low and somehow distant.

'What do you mean?'

'I can't protect him now. The pack's honour is at stake and if we don't bring him back, they will.'

'But you lead the pack, you control them.'

'Barely. They are restless; there are challengers. And they will not be satisfied until Rhydian has begged forgiveness and sworn his allegiance.'

Jana had a sudden idea. 'But he could do that, *here*.'

Alric stared. 'What do you mean?'

'What if he comes to you here, in the woods, and bows down before you and admits his mistakes? I would bear witness; that would satisfy the pack.'

Jana waited as her father considered her words. He seemed to be wavering.

'Then you and I can return to the pack, Dad,' she added urgently. 'And honour would be restored.'

Alric nodded slowly and then fixed his eyes on his daughter. 'You have until sundown.'

Ten

Jana knew it would not be easy. The old wolf and the young wolf, both strong and proud, both certain they were in the right. She'd have to use all her natural cunning to bring them together and then convince Rhydian that he must bow down and swear his allegiance to Alric and the pack. Rhydian knew the ways of the pack and the laws and rituals but accepting them did not come easily or naturally. Before being accepted by Maddy's family and then the wild Wolfblood pack, he had lived most of his life as an outsider, a lone wolf. So it was not merely a case of reminding him of his duty and obligations, he had to be convinced it was the right thing to do.

There was no time to speak before the first lesson after lunch, which was English literature, where the class were working on Shakespeare's play *Romeo and Juliet*. The plot of the ancient grudge between two warring families suddenly seemed particularly relevant to Jana, Rhydian and even Maddy, especially as they learned that the love between Romeo and Juliet ultimately led the families to realise the only way forward was through reconciliation and forgiveness.

As passages of the dialogue were read aloud Jana glanced at Rhydian and saw that he was deep in thought. Maddy looked thoughtful too, as though there was much on her mind.

And Rhydian and Jana discovered exactly what Maddy was worrying about when she called them to one side after the lesson. 'Look, I heard you talking about Alric earlier,' she admitted, 'and I know he's back. I know I should apologise for listening in, but I'm not sorry I heard. Stay away from him, Rhydian.'

Maddy was half expecting a furious outburst from Jana after her confession but her response was calm and controlled. 'My dad's not the problem now,' she said, 'it's the pack. If Rhydian doesn't bow to Alric, they'll all come back. Then you and your family will be targets, and who knows what they'll do if they find out Tom and Shannon know Wolfblood secrets.'

Jana's words seemed to be spurring Rhydian towards a decision. 'But Alric says if I make my peace with him, and apologise, then he'll forgive her and she can go home,' he said to Maddy. 'And then I'll be able to see my own family again too.'

'But Alric tried to kill you before.' Maddy was still

not convinced. 'Why should you trust him now?'

The three young Wolfbloods fell silent as Tom and Shannon joined them. No one said a word and the long silence became embarrassing.

Jana nodded to Maddy. 'You'd better tell them, it affects them too.'

'Us?' Shannon asked. 'What does?'

Maddy wasted no words as she briefly outlined the situation to Tom and Shannon, who listened intently, their faces becoming more and more grave.

'So, what now?' Tom said when Maddy had told all.

'I'll do it,' Rhydian said shortly. 'Not just for Jana or for me, for all of us. So that this can be over.' He looked at Maddy. 'So that you and your family don't have to live in fear of them and maybe I'll get to see my family again one day.'

'Can we come with you?' Maddy asked. 'To make sure you're all right?'

Rhydian shook his head. 'No. This is between me and Alric.'

Each step Rhydian and Jana took through the woodland carried them closer to their meeting with Alric and closer to the moment when they would have to say goodbye.

'I'm really going to miss all this,' Jana muttered.

'You mean us?'

Jana nodded. 'Everything.'

'It's not forever though,' Rhydian said, 'not if your dad keeps his word.'

'He will.'

Alric had told Jana he would be waiting for them in the cover of a hollow. They climbed a small incline and as they crested the ridge they saw the pack leader standing beneath the overhanging branches of a large tree.

He looked stern and unforgiving as he stared at Rhydian. 'Well, well, well, you've got more guts than I thought.'

'Don't be like that, Dad,' Jana said. 'He's come to beg for your forgiveness.'

'Then he'd better get on with it.' He pointed to the ground and glared at Rhydian. 'Submit!'

Rhydian looked at Jana. He hated hearing the words 'submit' and 'beg', but he had given his word. Slowly he crouched down, lowered his head, and began muttering the ancient Wolfblood words of submission.

Alric grinned triumphantly and then threw back his head and gave a long howl of victory.

It was a signal. With a terrifying roar, a second wild Wolfblood dropped from the branches and snared Rhydian in a heavy rope net, catching him completely unawares.

The second Wolfblood was Aran, Alric's closest and

most loyal follower. He sprang to his feet, pulling the net tighter as Rhydian struggled and wriggled, barely able to move.

Jana was horrified. 'No, Dad!' she screamed. 'You said he wouldn't be hurt!'

Alric glared. 'You'd really defend this worthless boy against me?' he snarled. 'I am your father!'

'And he is my friend! This is not what we agreed!'

'Finally he will be punished and the pack will fear me again!' Alric's eyes gleamed yellow and he laughed loudly. 'I have come for Rhydian's pelt!'

'No! You can't do this! I won't let you!'

Alric signalled to Aran, who had a second heavy net. 'Then in that, case, you will be dragged back to the pack as well!'

With Rhydian completely helpless, Aran advanced on Jana, preparing to throw the net, and in the same instant Maddy came hurtling into the hollow, a thick fallen branch clasped in both hands. She swung it at Aran's legs with all her strength. He howled in pain and crashed to the ground.

Alric roared furiously and lurched towards Maddy, but Jana leapt at her father, gripping him tightly around the neck. Maddy grabbed the second net and threw it over the groaning Aran, and as he rolled on the ground he became trapped in the heavy mesh.

Jana was not strong enough to hold her father for long. He threw her down and strode ferociously towards Maddy. 'You!' he growled. 'You think you're a match for a real Wolfblood?'

Maddy was afraid but determined not to show it. She told herself to be strong, stronger than she'd ever been before. 'You're just a desperate *old* wolf,' she snarled. 'Clinging to power. Well, you don't scare me, not any more.'

Enraged, Alric's eyes flashed yellow and his veins began to throb and bulge. But Maddy would not back down and as the wild Wolfblood transformed into wolf form, she did the same.

Within seconds the two wolves were facing each other, snarling, staring, waiting for the moment to attack. They circled warily, preparing for a fight to the death.

The sun had gone completely; night had descended on the woodland. Two lights flashed, momentarily flickering over the canopy, and then Tom and Shannon came racing into the clearing by torchlight. Wolf-Alric was distracted as he watched them rush to Rhydian and begin freeing him from the net.

When wolf-Alric looked back at wolf-Maddy he saw that she was not alone. Jana had transformed too and was glaring and snarling with her fangs bared. Now it was two against one and seconds later it was three, as Rhydian transformed.

In the other net, Aran was battling to free himself but was forced to give up the struggle as Tom and Shannon ran over and sat on him.

Wolf-Alric growled and edged forward, preparing to launch himself at the three younger wolves. But then he howled in frustration. His chance had gone, the odds against victory were too heavy; the battle was over – and lost.

Slowly he backed away, cowering, whining, and then he retransformed into human form, watching mournfully as his daughter and her friends did the same.

'You sided with them! Over *me*!' he snarled at his daughter before glaring at Tom and Shannon. 'And with *humans*!'

'They're my friends. Why did you have to lie to me?'

'I was trying to protect you!'

Tom and Shannon stood up and backed away as Alric strode over and freed Aran from the net. He snarled ferociously at the two humans, who had dared to keep him trapped, but it was all bluster: the fight was gone from the wild Wolfbloods now.

Alric cast a final look at his daughter. 'There's no way back for you.' His words were both sad and bitter. 'You're no daughter of mine. Not any more.'

And with that, the two wild Wolfbloods ran off into the night.

Soon, only the sound of Jana's sobbing broke the silence.

Eleven

The mood inside the Land Rover as it trundled along winding country roads towards the sea was mostly as bright as the early spring morning. Shannon and Tom were enthusiastically joining in a game of linking song titles with Daniel and Emma. Only Maddy looked less than completely happy.

'"I Left My Heart in San Francisco",' Daniel said as he drove.

'"Don't Break My Heart",' Emma chipped in, keeping the heart theme going.

'"Heartbreaker"!' Shannon said.

Tom was thinking hard.

'Five seconds, Tom,' Shannon said, looking at her watch. 'Four . . . three . . .'

'"You Took My Heart"!'

They waited for Maddy's contribution. She glared into her dad's eyes, which were reflected back at hers in the rear-view mirror and said quietly, '"I Knew I Couldn't Trust You".'

Daniel sighed. 'That is not a song title for a start.'

'Er . . . it is actually,' Tom said. 'Silverstein.'

Emma turned in the passenger seat to speak to her daughter. 'Look, we've told you, it wasn't our fault, love.'

'Social services made the decision,' Daniel added hurriedly.

'But you didn't mention it until the very last minute,' Maddy said angrily.

'We didn't know,' Emma said. 'Not for certain, not until just before you did.'

The decision had taken Maddy and Rhydian completely by surprise. Just when he was settling happily into life with the Smith family, word had come through that he was to return to his official foster parents. He had moved back in with Mr and Mrs Vaughan the previous day.

'Cheer up, eh, pet?' Emma continued. 'Don't let it ruin our day out.'

'But he wanted to come with us.'

'He has to get to know the Vaughans again. He can come for Sunday lunch, tomorrow. How's that?'

Maddy sighed but then nodded and immediately sent a text to Rhydian passing on her mum's invitation for the following day. She received a smiley face reply a few seconds later.

But her dad's face had lost its grin. 'I've got a feeling we took a wrong turn a few miles back.'

'We?' Emma said.

'All right, I.'

'Does that mean we're lost?'

'I thought Wolfbloods never got lost?' Shannon couldn't resist asking.

'Doesn't apply when we're driving,' Daniel told her.

Emma pointed ahead. 'Look, there's a garage, we can ask directions there.'

Daniel grinned. 'You're a genius.'

The little service station was old and dilapidated, very different from the modern, high-tech versions located on busy roads or by supermarkets. A paint-flaked sign over the kiosk door read, *The Mottled Poppy.*

Daniel brought the Land Rover to a standstill alongside an ancient, rusting petrol pump and got out, followed by Maddy, Tom and Shannon. They all made their way into the kiosk while Emma stayed to fill the petrol tank.

Standing behind the counter was a grey-haired, smiling man who looked to be in his sixties. 'Going somewhere nice?' he called to Maddy and her friends as they looked over the sweets for sale.

'Blackpool,' came the reply from Maddy.

'But we've got ourselves a bit lost,' Daniel added as he approached the counter, carrying a road map.

'You don't have a satnav, then?' the man asked.

'Never had to use one.' Daniel placed the road map on the counter. 'I think we took a wrong turn by the A66.'

A large mottled poppy in a pot sat on the counter and Daniel moved it to one side so that he could fully unfold the map. He looked down, trying to work out exactly where they were and hoping for some advice on the route to take, but when he glanced up at the man he saw he was staring, wide-eyed, at the poppy. Spots of colour were appearing on the petals.

Daniel laughed. 'What will they think of next? Is it electronic?'

'No, it's . . . it's . . .' the man muttered, almost as though he were in some sort of trance. 'It's real . . . a local thing.' He looked closely at Daniel. 'Will you excuse me for a moment?'

'Everything all right?'

'Yes, it's the, er . . . the petrol pump, it's playing up. Overcharging. I'll sort it out. And I, er . . . I didn't like the sound of your vehicle as you pulled in.'

'Really? I didn't notice.'

The man hurried to the door just as Emma came in. 'Have some coffee. On the house,' he said as he pushed by.

Outside, he pulled an old mobile phone from a pocket and punched in a number. The call was answered quickly.

'You'll never guess what,' the man said. 'The poppy changed colour!'

Rhydian had quickly become bored with reacquainting himself with the Vaughans. They were an extremely nice and caring couple but had little in common with the teenager they were fostering.

So as soon as he could, Rhydian made his excuses and went to find Jana. A little later they were walking together in the woodland, both feeling far more at home than when they were cooped up indoors.

They came to a shallow but wide stream, which could be crossed by a series of flat stones sitting just above the surface of the water.

Using her Wolfblood skills, Jana effortlessly skipped across the stones, reaching the far side without getting even a foot wet. 'Your turn,' she said, grinning back at Rhydian.

'No worries.'

He jumped to the first and then the second stone without a problem, but as he landed on the third he felt something slip from his jacket pocket. There was a splashing sound and Rhydian looked back to see his mobile phone in the water. 'Oh no.'

Fishing the phone from the water was no problem, but there was no sign of life when Rhydian tried to restart it. 'I don't think my smartphone is very smart any more,' he said with a sigh.

'It's strange how you all depend on those things,' Jana said. 'If I want to know what the weather's going to be like I look at the sky.'

'Yeah, but in the human world, if you really want to fit in you need one of these.' He held up the phone. 'When they work, that is.'

'I prefer the natural world,' Jana said. 'Let's go to the Howling Tree.'

'The what?'

'I found it. I'll show you.'

It was not far. Jana had discovered a huge, long-dead tree, with a hollow trunk. Close to the bottom, part of the trunk had rotted away. Jana crouched down, took a deep breath and let out a long howl into the trunk. The sound reverberated around the old wood and Jana howled again, higher this time, and the two sounds mingled so that the notes that finally echoed away across the woodland were strangely beautiful.

Soon they were both howling into the tree, creating weird and wonderful Wolfblood music. When they finally stopped, the last howling echoes faded to a strange and eerie silence.

'Amazing,' Rhydian said.

Jana did not reply and when Rhydian looked at her she appeared to be close to tears.

'What's wrong?'

'I can never go back to the wild now. Can I?'

'You didn't have a choice, not after the way your dad behaved.'

'But . . .' Jana hesitated, but she had to blurt out the truth. 'Rhydian, when I came here, it wasn't because my father threw me out. He told me to come and bring you back. I'm sorry.'

'So . . . so you were lying to me? The whole time?'

'I'm sorry. I knew that if I didn't do it, you'd never return to us.' She started to move towards Rhydian but he backed away. 'Please don't hate me, please. If I'm going to live here, you had to know the truth. My father promised you'd come to no harm, but he lied. And now I've chosen you over my kin, my pack, over everything. Your world is all I've got now, Rhydian.'

She was right; Rhydian knew that. And he knew also that Jana standing alongside him and Maddy to cour-ageously face the fury of Alric had been the difference between life and death.

He nodded. 'It's OK, and I'm sorry. Every day us Wolfbloods keep our secret from the world. But we can't do that if there are secrets between us.'

'I know. And from now on, no more secrets and no more lies.'

They walked on through the wood and it was obvious to Rhydian that there was something more on Jana's mind. 'Can I ask you something?' she said at last.

'If you want.'

'It's . . . it's Maddy's parents.'

'What about them?'

'They've lived among humans forever, right?'

'Yeah . . .?'

'So every full moon, when they're wolf, how is it they've never been caught?'

Rhydian stopped walking and thought for a moment. Then he smiled and took a key from his jacket pocket. 'Well, since we're sharing secrets now, I'll show you.'

The bonnet was up and the garage owner had his head in the engine compartment. 'Try her again,' he called to Daniel, who turned the ignition key. The starter motor whirred but the engine failed to cough into life.

'I don't understand,' Daniel called from the driver's seat. 'It always starts.'

'I knew something was wrong when you pulled in. I'm pretty sure it's the alternator.'

Daniel was no great mechanic. 'That sounds serious.'

Maddy and the others were standing by the kiosk. Tom, Shannon and Emma were anxious to be on the move again, but Maddy was busy with her phone. 'Why's he not answering?'

Tom shrugged. 'Maybe his phone's died.'

'Give it a rest, love,' Emma said impatiently.

'What?' Maddy said, looking up from her phone.

'You're on a day out with your friends and all you can do is text Rhydian.'

'So?'

'You're acting as though he's your boyfriend. Is he your boyfriend, then?'

'What? No!'

Emma did not seem convinced. 'You could have fooled me. Both of us, actually.' She was about to continue but stopped herself, thinking that maybe she had already said too much.

'It was *you*,' Maddy breathed as realisation struck. 'It wasn't social services who wanted Rhydian back with the Vaughans, was it? It was you and Dad.'

Emma hesitated; the truth was out. 'Look, Rhydian's a nice lad, but he's not *our* lad.' She glanced over to the vehicle to make sure the garage owner was not listening. 'He's in our pack, not our family. We just didn't want you two getting too close; sometimes it seems as though you are'.

'So you thought you'd just chuck him out instead of talking to me about it?' Maddy was furious.

'We did what we thought best. For both of you.'

'I bet you've been planning it for weeks. Talking to the Vaughans and social services. And never a word.'

'We didn't want to upset you.'

'So how do you think I feel now?' She turned away, looking to Tom and Shannon for support. But they kept silent, wary of being drawn into the argument.

The Land Rover's bonnet clanged shut. 'I keep a lot of spare parts in my workshop at home,' the garage owner said to Daniel. 'There could be a spare alternator there; we'll go and take a look.'

'Oh, I couldn't possibly ask you to do that.'

'It's no trouble; I was closing up anyway. And you can't drive this without an alternator. I'll give you a tow.'

'But . . .'

The man held out his right hand. 'The name's Bob Driscoll.'

Twelve

The sign on the ancient stone gatepost read HARFIRE
HALL and after negotiating the long driveway the two
vehicles came to a standstill outside an impressively large
country house nestling in extensive grounds.

'Garage business must be good,' Daniel said to Bob
Driscoll as he emerged from the Land Rover, followed
by Emma, Shannon, Tom and Maddy.

'My wife Mary's the housekeeper. Before Lord Harfire
left us he put a clause in his will protecting her job.'

As Mr Driscoll spoke, a smiling woman bustled through
the tall front door and down the wide stone steps.

'Ah, Mary, dear,' Bob Driscoll said, 'here are our waifs
and strays.'

Mrs Driscoll greeted the newcomers like long-lost
friends and then ushered them into the house, where she
insisted on taking their coats so they would be more
comfortable. The high-ceilinged house was dark and
gloomy, with heavy furniture and walls covered with
massive, gilt-framed oil paintings.

Shannon lingered in the hallway in front of a huge, dark portrait, which, judging by the clothes of the man posing with a gun in one hand and a flaming torch in the other, must have been well over two hundred years old. Shannon peered closely at the painting. A full moon cast an eerie silver light high above the man's head. He wore a poppy in one lapel and on the bottom of the frame was a heraldic shield with another poppy alongside the title of the painting, which was *Reclaim the Moonlight*.

Shannon craned her head to peer even more closely. In the background, cloaked in darkness, were the silhouettes of several cowering wolves, their yellow eyes glittering in the moonlight. Shannon shivered; the painting was definitely creepy.

'Coat?'

Shannon wheeled around. Mrs Driscoll was standing there beaming at her, a coat hanger in one hand.

'I'm all right, thanks, and . . .'

'Oh no, can't have you catching a chill when you go outside again.' Mrs Driscoll was removing Shannon's coat as she spoke. 'There. Now, you come through to the drawing room with the others.'

Shannon followed obediently as Mr Driscoll led everyone into the drawing room. Most of the furniture was covered in dustsheets but a huge log fire blazed in the hearth. Tom instinctively went towards it to warm his hands, but Daniel, Emma and Maddy all tensed and backed away. Open fire meant danger to Wolfbloods.

Bob Driscoll was watching them closely. 'I love a nice fire, don't you?'

'Actually, I'm a bit hot,' Daniel said.

'Yeah, me too,' Emma added.

Tom had remembered why the Smiths were suddenly uneasy and attempted to draw attention away from the fire. He'd noticed an ancient and unusual gun resting on a stand, the end of the barrel splayed, like the bell of a trumpet. 'Does that thing work?' he asked Mr Driscoll.

'Oh yes, it's a blunderbuss.'

'What does it fire?'

'Shot, musket balls, anything really. It's the traditional Harfire hunting gun. Though it hasn't been used since the last Lord Harfire was . . . taken.'

'Taken?' Daniel said. 'You mean he died?'

'No, no, taken to . . . to a home. They thought he was mad. But he wasn't.'

Shannon was feeling decidedly uneasy, having recognised the gun as the one in the portrait. And matters didn't improve when she glimpsed what looked like an animal skin pushed under a side table.

The feeling of unease seemed to be catching. Daniel

wanted to get away from the fire and the peculiar situation they had found themselves in. 'Can we take a look at the Land Rover now?'

'Of course,' Mr Driscoll said, smiling.

Emma needed to get out too. 'I could use the bathroom.'

'Follow me.'

As they left the room, Shannon held Tom and Maddy back and guided them to the side table. Stooping down, she tentatively gripped the animal skin and pulled it partly into view. It was a folded wolf pelt with the head still attached.

Maddy reeled back in horror and had to stop herself from screaming.

'She must have hidden it before we arrived,' Shannon breathed.

'Who did?'

'Mrs Driscoll. I think they know, Mads.'

'Know what?'

'That you're Wolfbloods.'

'How can they possibly know?'

'There's something strange here. Come and see the picture in the hall.'

They went through to the gloomy hall and stared up at the towering, threatening painting of the mad Lord

Harfire's ancestor. Maddy's keen eyes quickly picked out the shapes of wolves in the background.

'I think we should check out this place online,' she said. 'I'll get my phone, it's in my coat.'

But when she went to the nearby cloakroom there was no sign of any of the coats.

'What is going on?' Tom said, alarmed. 'Looks like they don't want us to leave.'

'I'm getting Dad,' Maddy said.

'And we'll look for the coats,' Shannon said.

Maddy hurried outside to the Land Rover but her dad was not there, and neither was Mr Driscoll. As she went to turn away, Maddy glanced into the vehicle and spotted Shannon's laptop on the back seat. She knew Shannon wouldn't mind her using it.

In less than a minute Maddy had powered up the laptop and found what she was looking for. She read aloud from a webpage. '*Harfire Hall is home to the legend of the Mottled Poppy. Dating from the Middle Ages, the legend says that the poppies grown on the estate are capable of detecting . . . werewolves.*' Maddy scrolled down the page further and read the ancient legend printed in bold. '*When the spots appear, the wolf is near.*'

Maddy looked up, hearing the crunch of footsteps on

the gravel driveway. It was her mum. 'Where is everyone?' Emma asked as she opened the door.

'Mam, you'd better look at this.'

Maddy shuffled across the seat so that her mum could sit next to her. It took only moments for Emma to see that they were in a terribly dangerous situation. 'Right,' she said, 'we're going. Get the coats.'

'I can't, they've gone.'

'Gone where?'

Maddy shrugged. 'Tom and Shannon went looking for them.'

'Well, we're leaving anyway. Somehow. Save that page so we can show your dad.' Emma glanced around the deserted driveway. 'When we can find your dad.'

Maddy saved the page but then noticed a group of files on the laptop, each named *Wolfblood*, followed by a number.

'Mam . . .' Maddy breathed as she opened *Wolfblood 1*.

Maddy and her mother stared with mounting horror as much of their life as Wolfbloods was revealed on Shannon's laptop screen. There were video files and hundreds of thumbnail shots taken from the camera hidden in the owl in the den.

'All our secrets,' Emma whispered, barely able to

believe what she was seeing. 'How could she do this to us?'

Just as they spoke, Shannon came hurrying from the house. 'There is something not right here,' she said quickly. 'Tom and I just . . .' She stopped and stared as she saw her laptop resting on Maddy's lap.

'You lying sneak!' Maddy snarled.

'All this time,' Emma growled, equally ferociously. 'You've been spying on us!'

'It's . . . it's to protect you!' Shannon looked petrified. 'Sooner or later people will find out and they'll spread lies.' She pointed at the laptop. 'That tells the truth. I didn't mean any harm, truly I didn't. I'd forgotten the camera was even there.'

'Oh, really,' Maddy said, looking at the screen again. 'So what's this, *live link*, then?'

She clicked on the link and the laptop connected remotely to the webcam hidden in the owl. Grainy black and white images of Jana pacing around the den came into view.

'She's there!' Maddy gasped. 'Now!'

'What is *she* doing in *my* house?' Emma demanded.

'I . . . I don't know,' Shannon groaned.

There was no sound but it was not necessary. The pictures told the story as a grinning Rhydian came into view with a plateful of meat he must have taken from the fridge.

Maddy was almost in tears. She looked from the screen to her mum, to Shannon and then back at the screen. 'Everyone,' she said. 'All of you. Lying, just lying all the time.'

'Tea's ready!' Mrs Driscoll was on the steps, smiling down at them. 'There's homemade cake too. I'd love to know what you think of it.'

Shannon leaned into the car, grabbed the laptop and slammed it shut as Maddy turned away in disgust.

'Actually, we really need to be going,' Emma said to Mrs Driscoll.

'But the car's not fixed.'

'We'll sort it, somehow, and we're not hungry. Or thirsty. And where's my husband?'

'With mine, I suppose.' Mrs Driscoll looked highly put out. 'And there's no need to be uncivil.'

'I'm sorry, but we have to be going. There's a problem at home.'

'Very well,' Mrs Driscoll said. 'You'd better follow me.'

She led them into the house, along a narrow corridor and then down a long flight of stone stairs. 'I expect they're down here,' Mrs Driscoll said, her voice loud as it bounced off the stone walls. 'Bob keeps all his old spare parts down here.'

They turned a corner and came face to face with Bob Driscoll, who must have heard their approach. He was blocking the way to the cellar room.

'Bob, the family have some sort of crisis at home. They have to leave now. Did you find the spare part in there?'

Mr Driscoll looked flustered, as though he'd been caught out. 'Er . . . yes,' he said, trying to regain his composure. 'Daniel's . . . er . . . he's looking at it now. Come on in.'

He stepped aside to allow Emma, Maddy and Shannon to pass and go into a large cellar.

'Daniel!' Emma gasped. Daniel was slumped on the floor at the far end of the room. He was chained to the wall and appeared to be unconscious. Tom was at his side, chained too, and gagged. Emma ran to her husband as Maddy and Shannon were violently shoved into the room. As they staggered and almost fell, the heavy barred door clanged shut and the key turned in the lock.

Thirteen

The Driscolls were ecstatic, joyously congratulating each other as they viewed their prisoners though the barred door.

'Got you! Got you all, and we know who you are,' Mary Driscoll bragged. 'And after next week's full moon, the whole world will know too. The public and the press will gather to see you change.'

'Change into what?' Maddy yelled. 'We're just people, like you.'

'You're not people, you're beasts!'

Bob Driscoll gleefully quoted the old legend. 'When the spots appear, the wolf is near!' He grinned at Emma and pointed at Daniel. 'I watched them appear when he came into my garage.'

'Make yourself comfortable for now,' Mrs Driscoll laughed. 'Enjoy your stay.'

Shannon ran to the bars as the Driscolls turned to leave. 'Wait!' she called. 'Listen to me.'

'We have nothing more to say to werewolves.'

'But I'm not a werewolf,' Shannon shouted. 'I'm a werewolf hunter too. Look, I can prove it.' She opened her laptop as the Driscolls hesitated. 'I've been hunting them for years, like you. Look!'

'Pass it through the bars,' Mr Driscoll said.

'No way.' Shannon clutched the laptop to her chest. 'You're not walking off with my evidence.'

'Shannon, what are you doing?' Maddy said, horrified.

But Shannon ignored her friend. 'Please,' she said to Mr Driscoll. 'They'll kill me if you leave me here, and then destroy all my evidence.'

The Driscolls exchanged a look and then swiftly unlocked the door and pulled Shannon through. Before Maddy could react, the door was slammed shut and the key turned in the lock.

As Shannon was led away, Maddy yelled after her, 'You traitor! I'll never forgive you, never!'

'Maddy,' Emma hissed. 'Don't waste your breath. Help Tom.'

Tom sucked in large gulps of air as soon as Maddy removed the gag. 'Thanks, Mads.' He gestured with his head to a broken mug on the floor. 'They must have drugged Daniel's tea with something. I heard him groaning and came in and the next thing I remember was coming round with the gag in my mouth.' He groaned. 'My head hurts.'

Daniel was gradually regaining consciousness. Emma held his head gently in her hands as his eyelids flickered and then opened. 'Hello,' he said weakly.

'How could Shannon do this to us?' Maddy said. Tom shifted uncomfortably against the wall. 'You don't really believe she's siding with them, do you?'

'But she's been spying on us! All this time!'

Tom nodded. 'I know.'

'You know! You too!'

'I found out. I wanted her to tell you. Look, Mads, Shan wouldn't share the info she's got with anyone.'

'She sharing it with *them*! Now!'

Up in the drawing room, Bob Driscoll placed his keys on the side table and beckoned to Shannon to come closer to the fire. She strode over, unafraid, and stood close to the roaring flames.

Driscoll nodded as his wife approached Shannon with a mottled poppy in a pot. Shannon leaned towards the poppy but the leaves remained exactly the same.

Mrs Driscoll nodded to her husband. 'She's human.'

Mr Driscoll was delighted. He pointed at the laptop. 'Now show us what you've got.'

Shannon opened several of the Wolfblood files and the Driscolls gazed in awe at the photos and videos.

'Amazing,' Bob Driscoll breathed. 'Incredible. We'll convince the doubters once and for all.'

'Why do you call them Wolfbloods?' Mrs Driscoll asked Shannon as she watched her open another file.

Shannon shrugged. 'It's just a pet name really. I've got some of their wolf hair in my bag. Would you like to see it?'

'Oh yes,' Mr Driscoll said as he gazed in wonder at the laptop.

'It's in the car. I'll get it while you watch this next file. You can see them changing from human to werewolf, it's incredible.'

She clicked on the file and the video started. The Driscolls stared, transfixed by the images on the laptop as Shannon walked from the room, snatching the keys from the side table as she went.

Shannon was perfectly calm as she unlocked the door to the cellar and then ran over to free first Daniel and then Tom.

'I knew you'd come back for us,' Tom said as the shackles fell from his wrist.

Daniel got unsteadily to his feet. 'Where are they?'

'Upstairs. We have to be quick and quiet,' Shannon told him.

They moved noiselessly from the cellar and up the stone staircase.

'The car,' Emma breathed to her husband. 'What do we do?'

'There's nothing wrong with it,' Daniel said. 'He just pulled a couple of leads free so it wouldn't start. At least I hope he did.'

Outside, as Daniel opened up the bonnet to search for the problem, Shannon turned to go back into the house.

'Shannon, where are you going?' Maddy hissed.

'To get my laptop.'

'No, you can't!'

'You want to leave it with them?'

She didn't wait for an answer and went hurrying up the steps. But in the drawing room the Driscolls were not as unprepared as Shannon was hoping. They had heard footsteps on the gravel, and while Mr Driscoll stood loading the old blunderbuss his wife watched with the laptop clutched in both hands.

They heard the Land Rover cough into life; Daniel had got it started. Mr Driscoll went charging past Shannon as she rushed towards Mrs Driscoll.

'Give me that,' Shannon snarled.

'Never!'

Mrs Driscoll tried to back away but stumbled on the

wolf pelt sticking out from beneath the side table. As she struggled to keep her balance, Shannon lunged forward and in one quick move had grabbed the laptop and was running from the room.

As Shannon tore down the steps she saw Mr Driscoll pointing the ancient blunderbuss at the Land Rover and preparing to fire. Shannon didn't hesitate. She barged into the werewolf hunter, sending him and the blunderbuss flying.

As Mr Driscoll scrabbled on the ground to retrieve the weapon, Shannon leapt into the open back door and the Land Rover hurtled away down the drive.

Fourteen

The trip to Blackpool forgotten, the Smith family drove back to Stoneybridge in virtual silence, everyone stunned by what had happened. It had been a narrow escape; they knew they had come closer than ever before to having their Wolfblood secrets revealed to the world. But they were safe again, for the time being. The Driscolls could do nothing more without evidence.

Once at the house, Maddy went straight down into the den and ripped the wooden owl from the ceiling. She was about to smash the hidden camera when Shannon came in and snatched it away.

'I'll take that.'

'Want to spy on someone else now, do you?'

'It's mine, and I want it, that's all.'

'You have to delete everything you have about us on your laptop!'

'I've already explained, Maddy,' Shannon snapped, 'to you and to your parents.' She was getting tired of having to justify her actions, even though she knew full well she had been invading the Smith family's privacy. 'People like the Driscolls think you're monsters; everything on my laptop proves you're not. It's insurance, for you all.'

Maddy couldn't see it that way and was not about to change her mind. 'I want you to get rid of it, Shannon, erase it completely.'

Shannon shook her head. 'You should learn to trust, Maddy.'

'I trusted you, and look where it got me.'

The argument raged on until Shannon left that evening. When they met at school the following Monday they hardly spoke and after that they deliberately avoided each other. Maddy felt betrayed and hurt. The trust was gone. Shannon was her oldest and closest friend and suddenly it seemed she hardly knew her at all.

And then there was Rhydian. He'd let her down as well by going into the den and sharing its secrets with Jana while the house was empty. In a furious outburst Maddy demanded he hand back his key to the house.

'Maddy, what's wrong with you?' Rhydian asked, taking the key from his pocket.

'Maybe I'm just sick of people doing things behind my back!' She grabbed the key and stormed off.

Everything felt strange for Maddy. Things were changing and she couldn't control them. Even Tom, good, loyal, faithful Tom, had kept secret the fact that he knew Shannon had been spying on the Wolfblood family.

The atmosphere between the friends was tense. Maddy hardly said a word to Jana and completely ignored Shannon. And it wasn't much better with Rhydian, especially as he seemed to be getting closer and closer to Jana. Shannon did everything she could – short of erasing the footage on her laptop, despite Maddy's demands – to make things up with her best friend, but it got her nowhere. So after a while she switched to becoming friendlier with Jana, who was suspicious at first, but gradually softened. Rhydian felt torn between the two Wolfblood girls while Tom . . . was Tom, constantly trying to be the best of friends to them all.

They were in a science class, everyone in pairs, apart from Maddy, who had very deliberately chosen to work alone.

Shannon was with Tom, when Rhydian came over and spoke quietly. He'd decided he had to step in. 'Don't you think it's time you and Maddy made up?' he said to Shannon.

'She won't listen.'

104

'But it's this . . . *research* of yours, Shannon, on the laptop. If you'd –'

'I saved her life.'

'Yeah, I know, we all know. But if that stuff fell into the wrong hands . . .'

'It won't, Rhydian.'

Tom was just as concerned as Rhydian. 'Imagine how Jana would flip if she found out you'd been spying on Wolfbloods, Shan?'

Shannon glanced across the room to Jana and then leaned closer to Rhydian. 'Maddy hasn't told her?'

'Course not. Jana would probably eat you!'

'But Jana's not stupid,' Tom added. 'She asked me why you'd fallen out with Maddy.'

'What did you say?' Shannon looked decidedly worried.

Tom shrugged. 'Girls' stuff.'

'And what does that mean?'

Tom shrugged again. 'I dunno, it was all I could think of.'

A few days later, though, Jana did learn the truth about Shannon and her laptop.

The elections for the year representative on the school council were taking place and Jimi Chen was standing. In a bid to gain extra votes Jimi started offering cash to anyone who voted for him. Shannon heard about it and took secret photographs and Jimi was thrown out of the election.

Mr Jeffries congratulated Shannon for her integrity in exposing the scam. But Maddy was not so pleased and could no longer hold her tongue when she saw Shannon in the playground. 'You?' she snapped. 'Integrity!'

'Jimi was bribing voters!' Shannon said as Rhydian and Jana joined them.

'Yeah, but two wrongs don't make a right!'

'Oh, and what did I do wrong?'

Maddy shook her head, apparently amazed that she had to explain. 'Spying on people with hidden cameras. Again!'

'Again?' Jana said. 'What do you mean, again?'

'It's nothing,' Rhydian said quickly. 'She doesn't mean anything.'

'No!' Maddy snapped. 'It's not nothing. Jana needs to know the truth; I've had enough of lies.'

'What lies?' Jana said. 'What are you talking about now?

Maddy looked at Shannon and then at Rhydian. 'Shannon's putting us all in danger. Including you!'

Once Jana had learned the truth, it was all that

Rhydian, Tom and Maddy could do to stop her from attacking Shannon, but somehow they kept her under control.

But there was no controlling her later when she cornered Shannon in the photocopying room. 'You're a liar and a traitor,' she snarled.

Panic-stricken, Shannon could see the familiar signs as Jana began to wolf out; the eyes turning yellow, the veins in her neck and the back of her hands starting to bulge and flow with dark, silver liquid.

'Jana,' she gasped, 'Jana, I'd never do anything to hurt you.'

'I was stupid ever to trust you. You're not a friend, you're a predator.'

The walls of the small room were lined with shelves, stacked high with boxes of stationery and packets of paper for photocopying.

Shannon reached forward to try to calm Jana but it was too late. The Wolfblood lashed out ferociously and Shannon stumbled back. She grabbed for one of the shelves to steady herself but the flimsy wooden structure was not fixed to the wall. The shelves tipped forward and fell, and as they smashed into the shelves on the other side the whole lot rocked and then collapsed.

Shannon sat on the floor, trapped behind a tangle of fallen shelves, boxes and paper. She could not and dare not move because on the other side of the tangled wreckage, Jana had wolfed out and was eyeing her malevolently, desperately trying to get through to her prey. But the wood and boxes were forming an effective barrier and wolf-Jana howled in frustration.

Across the school, Maddy and Rhydian heard the howl and immediately knew what had happened to Jana. Using their Wolfblood hearing and moving like lightning they were outside the room in seconds, knowing they had to act quickly before anyone else discovered the wolf in the cupboard. While Rhydian stood guard outside, Maddy went into the wolf's lair.

'Jana,' she said calmly, although her heart was thumping. 'Jana, I shouldn't have said anything. I know you're scared but please don't hurt Shannon. I know she wouldn't betray us. She'd never put you in danger, she's loyal and she's my friend, Jana. She's *our* friend.'

Wolf-Jana seemed to be calming, the aggression vanishing from her eyes.

'And she's in my pack, Jana, just like you,' Maddy continued. 'And nobody hurts my pack. So please, get control of it, I know you can do it. Come back to us.'

In the corridor outside there were voices and footsteps as others, drawn by the mysterious howling, came running up.

Mr Jeffries was among them. 'What's going on?' he said to Rhydian.

'It's . . . it's Jana, sir. The door got accidentally locked, and she's claustrophobic. I know what it's like, I suffer from it myself.'

'Yes, but that noise . . .?'

'What noise?'

'I . . .'

'Maddy's with her now, sir,' Rhydian said hurriedly. 'I think she's OK.'

'I'd better see for myself.' Mr Jeffries pushed past Rhydian into the photocopying room. It was a scene of complete devastation but Mr Jeffries, as always, was mostly concerned with the welfare of his students.

'Are you all right, Jana?' he asked gently.

Jana had returned to human form and was sitting on the floor. Maddy was next to her, with one arm around her shoulders.

Maddy looked up. 'She's fine now, sir. She just got scared, that's all.'

They got to their feet and Mr Jeffries led Jana away while Maddy helped Shannon through the tangle of wreckage. Maddy realised that as leader of the young members of her pack, she was responsible for keeping them together.

'Are you OK?' she asked as Shannon finally stepped clear of the boxes and broken shelves.

Shannon nodded and the two friends hugged tightly.

'I'm so sorry,' Maddy said. 'It's over now. It's over.'

There was no chance for Maddy to speak with Jana until school ended for the day. 'You saved me,' Jana said quietly as they walked towards the exit gates. 'And you saved Shannon too, and made me feel as though I belong as part of your pack.'

'Well, you are part of my pack,' Maddy told her.

Jana nodded. 'But . . .'

'What?'

'Well, as pack leader, what are you going to do about Shannon's laptop?'

Maddy sighed. 'Nothing.'

'So you're just going to leave it?'

'Shannon's in our pack too, Jana,' Maddy said firmly. 'I was wrong not to trust her before, so I won't make the same mistake again.'

Fifteen

Jimi Chen was in high spirits. His wealthy and well-connected dad had managed to pick up three top-price tickets for the one-off charity football match featuring an all-star international eleven playing a team of famous TV stars and celebrities.

It promised to be one of the games of the season, both for football fans and those thrilled by close encounters with celebrities. Jimi had been given all three tickets as a gift and the obvious next move would have been for him to hand over the spares to his two best mates, Liam Hunter and Sam Dodds. But as far as business was concerned, Jimi was just like his dad when sensing a good opportunity to make money.

So Liam and Sam were very welcome to the two extra tickets – as long as they could cough up one hundred pounds each. If not, there were many others at school desperate for a chance to buy the tickets, including the Three Ks, who wanted nothing more than to get up close to a couple of the soap stars lining up for the celebrity team. But a hundred pounds was a lot of money – unless you happened to be Jimi Chen.

Tom would have loved to be at the match, but a hundred pounds was way beyond what he could afford, so while others scrambled and schemed to come up with the cash, he stayed out of it.

Shannon wasn't interested. She had loyally cheered from the touchline on her one and only time at a football match, when Rhydian and Tom combined to lead the school to victory in the County Cup. But once was enough for Shannon.

Rhydian didn't mind the odd game of football, particularly when he could safely demonstrate his amazing ability to leap and make incredible saves when he played in goal, but he had no desire to watch a match, no matter who was playing.

Maddy wasn't bothered one way or another and could think of far more interesting things on which to spend a hundred pounds.

And as far as Jana was concerned, football was one of those totally pointless exercises only humans could have wasted their time in inventing. And besides, Jana's thoughts were still centred on something far more serious and potentially devastating than a game of football – the Wolfblood information stored on Shannon's laptop.

Despite Maddy's orders to leave well alone, Jana was convinced that the only way they could be safe was by deleting every last file, so she forced open Shannon's locker in a bid to snatch the laptop. But the locker was empty and Jana had to face up to Shannon's anger.

The following day disaster struck when the laptop went missing from Shannon's bag. She was certain that Jana was the culprit and before Maddy and Rhydian could stop her she went rifling through Jana's locker, but found nothing.

The Wolfbloods were once more in dreadful danger and the accusations and hostilities that Maddy had hoped were in the past returned with a vengeance. Tom had heard Maddy and Rhydian talking about the threat stored on the laptop and when he mentioned it to Shannon her suspicions switched to them. But another search proved fruitless.

The situation was rapidly approaching boiling point when the five young members of the Wolfblood pack met up in the photographic darkroom.

'I thought you took it,' Rhydian said to Jana.

'I did not take it!' Jana yelled. 'It was you.' She glared at Maddy. 'Or you!'

'It was not me!' Maddy said, struggling to stay calm. 'Or Rhydian!'

There was a tense silence as the five friends looked from one to another and considered the implications of what they had learned.

'So,' Tom said slowly, 'what we're agreeing now is that no one here has actually taken the laptop.' He paused for a moment. 'We are saying that, aren't we?'

They were standing in a tight circle.

Rhydian nodded. 'Yeah. Yeah, we are.'

'So that means someone else has got it,' Tom continued.

The full horror of the situation was dawning on them all. 'And all the Wolfblood research,' Maddy whispered.

'I told you!' Jana screamed. 'I told you this would happen!'

'What do we do?' Rhydian gasped.

'We find it,' Maddy said quickly. 'We find it!'

Jana was barely listening. 'We're dead! We are dead! Someone could be going through everything right now. All our secrets. We're dead!'

'I've got an idea!' Everyone turned to Shannon as she took out her phone. 'I've got GPS on my laptop, it's linked to my phone.'

'So you can track it?' Rhydian asked excitedly.

They waited anxiously as Shannon tried to locate the laptop via her phone but she shook her head. 'The laptop must be switched off; I can't locate it unless it's on.'

'Wait a minute,' Jana said suddenly. 'Liam!'

'What's he got to do with it?' Tom asked.

'Werewolves. All that stuff he told us about his ancestor killing a werewolf, when we knew it was a Wolfblood.'

'And my relative,' Maddy said.

Shannon nodded slowly as she realised where Jana was going with her thinking. 'Yes. Everyone knows about my old beast of the moors research. Maybe he's put two and two together and taken the laptop to see what else he can find.'

A few moments later, Liam found himself surrounded by the members of Maddy's pack.

'Got something you want to tell us, Liam?' Jana snarled.

Liam looked completely unruffled. 'Like, you're an idiot?'

Rhydian just about managed to stop Jana from leaping into an attack.

'Shannon's laptop,' Maddy said calmly.

'What?'

'We know you took it.'

'What are you on about? I haven't got her stupid laptop. It's a pile of junk! Why would I want that?'

Suddenly Shannon's phone bleeped. She hauled it quickly from a pocket. 'It's been switched on!'

Tom smiled weakly at Liam. 'Sorry, mate.'

It was slow progress. The laptop was definitely close by, somewhere in the school, but finding the precise location was tricky.

Shannon crossed the playground and then turned and set off in the opposite direction, with her phone held out in front of her.

They were getting closer and closer, the bleep of the tracking device getting louder and louder all the time. And then suddenly it stopped completely.

'What happened?' Maddy said.

Jana was already angry. 'You said you could track it.'

'The signal's gone! Maybe . . . maybe whoever's got it has uninstalled the app.'

They were close to the cluster of school buildings, with narrow walkways and little alleys running between them.

'We don't need an app!' Jana snarled. 'We're Wolfbloods!'

Moving at lightning speed, Jana leapt at the closest wall and climbed quickly to the roof. There was no chance of stopping her.

'Follow her scent,' Maddy said to Rhydian and they

set off at a run. Tom and Shannon could only follow more slowly.

Jana sped to the centre of the flat roof. She could see clearly in every direction. Engaging her Wolfblood hearing and sense of smell she paused, tracking her target more accurately than any GPS app could manage.

She had the scent, she was certain. She hurtled across the roof and in one flying leap crossed to another building. On the ground, Maddy and the others were racing to keep up.

Jana knew exactly where she was heading now. She reached the edge of the roof and peered over. Down below, in the narrow alleyway, a figure was crouched, staring at a laptop screen.

Jana jumped and landed noiselessly. 'You,' she breathed.

The laptop clattered to the ground.

Taken completely by surprise and totally confused, the thief stood up and turned to run in the opposite direction. Maddy and the others barred his way.

'You!' Shannon said. 'You took my laptop.'

'I . . . I . . .' Sam's face burned with shame. 'There was no way I could get a hundred quid.'

'So you thought you'd try to sell Shannon's laptop?' Tom said.

'I wouldn't have done it, really, I couldn't. As soon as I uninstalled the GPS I knew it was wrong.'

Shannon had grabbed the laptop to check it over. It was working, and none of her Wolfblood files were open. She nodded to the others.

Maddy sighed with relief. 'Let's go.'

Jana was staring at Sam. 'What? That's it? We just let him go?'

'What do you want to do, arrest him?'

'I want –'

'No, leave it,' Shannon said to Jana. She stared at Sam. 'He just made a stupid mistake.'

'I did,' Sam said quickly. 'I know I did. And I'm sorry, Shannon, really sorry. I'll never do anything like this again, I promise.'

Shannon could see that Sam meant what he said and realised that for all their sakes it would be best to let the matter drop. 'No, I don't think you will,' she said.

Sam turned to go but then glanced back. 'What's all that wolf stuff?'

'What?' Shannon's heart was thudding.

'I saw a folder . . . *Wolf Data*?'

'Oh that. It's just . . . just a project thing.'

Sam shrugged. 'Oh . . . oh, right. Sorry.'

The five friends breathed a collective sigh of relief as Sam slouched away. The Wolfbloods had come so close to disaster, yet again.

'I think you and me need to talk,' Maddy said to Shannon.

They went to the photography club darkroom, where Maddy knew they wouldn't be overheard.

'We almost lost everything,' she said as they sat facing each other.

'I know, and I promise it won't happen again.'

'But you can't promise that, Shan,' Maddy said urgently. 'We trusted you with our lives, our secrets, everything. You're meant to keep us safe.'

'I was keeping you safe. And I am. But I couldn't have known that Sam . . .'

'Yeah, that's the point, Shan. You can't protect us from something you can't see coming.'

'I can try.'

Maddy shook her head. 'I know this is difficult, Shan, but . . . you can either keep your research, or you can really keep your friends safe. Today's proved you can't do both.' Maddy stood up. 'I'll leave you to think about it. Talk to you tomorrow.'

'Wait,' Shannon said quickly.

Maddy watched as Shannon opened up her laptop.

She clicked on the *Wolfblood* folder and then looked at Maddy before pressing a key.

A box appeared on the screen. It read: ARE YOU SURE YOU WANT TO DELETE THESE FILES?

Shannon moved the curser again and selected YES.

The files slowly disappeared. All her research had gone. Forever.

Sixteen

With her precious and unique Wolfblood footage gone, Shannon felt as though part of herself was lost too. It had taken years to collect and collate but just a moment to delete and lose forever. She was miserable, and nothing Maddy said or did seemed to cheer her in the slightest.

Maddy spent days going through her own photograph albums to put together a scrapbook of the two of them over the years. And Shannon was politely grateful when Maddy gave her the scrapbook, but there was little real enthusiasm behind her words. Things just weren't the same.

It was the day of the school disco, organised by the Three Ks, who'd completely taken charge of the whole event, and managed to sell almost all the tickets. Tom was a big music fan and a wannabe DJ. He was really looking forward to a great night out, especially as Katrina had somehow managed to book the locally famous DJ Darby, whose weekly radio show was a must-listen for Tom.

At the start of the school day, Tom was really buzzing as he danced his way down the corridor. He reached Maddy, Rhydian and Jana, who were sitting on the floor, slumped against the lockers. They all looked dreadful – tired, washed out and thoroughly exhausted – the complete opposite to the highly energised Tom.

There was a reason for the Wolfbloods' lack of energy; it was the night of the dark of the moon, the time of the lunar month furthest from full moon, when Wolfbloods lost their powers and energy and wanted to do nothing more than sleep.

But Tom was too excited let his Wolfblood friends' lack of energy dampen his own enthusiasm. 'It's gonna be a great night, totally amazing. You're all coming, right?'

No one answered, so Tom tried again, targeting Jana, who looked the most tired of them all. 'You're up for it right, eh, Jana?' He did a few slick dance steps. 'Me and you?'

Jana just growled and Tom laughed and growled back, which at least made Maddy and Rhydian smile. But Maddy's smile disappeared as she saw Shannon approach, looking completely miserable.

Tom had spotted her and went hurrying over. 'Disco tonight, Shan, with DJ Darby! Are you coming?'

'Sorry, Tom,' Shannon replied, 'nothing in the world would make me go near that stupid disco.' She marched on, barely nodding at Maddy and the others.

The Ks were following, having shut up their ticket sales kiosk until lunchtime. And Katrina was bursting to tell her friends the hot news. 'I . . . am Harry Averwood's date for the disco.'

'Shut up!' Kara said, her eyes wide.

'A-ma-zing!' Kay added.

'Amazing, but true!' Katrina confirmed as they strutted onwards.

Harry Averwood was a sixth-former, lead guitarist in his own band, and generally regarded as one of the coolest guys in the school. Shannon had once sung with the band at the Stoneybridge Luna Fair, and her beautiful, soulful voice had impressed both Harry and the audience. But as she suffered from serious stage fright it had been a one-off occasion.

The three Wolfbloods struggled through morning lessons and were too weary to say anything to Shannon when she slipped quickly away. She wasn't in the mood for talking, even to her best friend Maddy.

Shannon knew how bad Maddy felt about persuading

her to delete her Wolfblood files, but she simply didn't want to talk about it any more. She wanted to be alone and found the perfect place as she passed one of the music department rehearsal rooms. It was deserted, so Shannon went inside, sat down and took out the scrapbook Maddy had given her. It was filled with great photographs of them both and after a few minutes Shannon found herself smiling as she turned the pages.

She didn't hear the door open. 'Shannon! What are you doing here?'

Shannon looked up. It was Harry Averwood carrying his guitar case. 'Harry! I . . . I just wanted a bit of time on my own.'

Harry was usually super-cool, but now he seemed unusually hesitant. 'I've . . . I've been thinking about you.'

'You . . . you have?'

'For this song I've written about . . . I mean, written *for* you. To sing, I mean. I think you'll be perfect for the vocals.'

'Me? Oh . . . I don't know . . .'

'I came to practise it and you're already here,' Harry said, smiling. 'It must be a sign, right?'

Shannon laughed. 'Well . . . maybe you're right. I'll give it a try.'

Harry took out his guitar and a lyrics sheet and then started picking the opening chords to the ballad he'd written. Soon they were singing together as Harry taught Shannon the melody. She was a quick learner and had soon mastered the tune.

'It sounds awesome,' Harry said as she sang the last line.

'It's a great song,' Shannon said modestly.

'You have an amazing voice, Shannon, you should do more with it.'

'You really think so?'

'Yes!'

They fell silent; both unsure of what to say next. Making music together had been much easier.

'So, are you going to the disco tonight?' Harry asked eventually.

'Don't think so.'

'Oh right, no worries, then.'

'Why did you ask?' Shannon said hesitantly.

'Well, you know Katrina . . .'

Shannon nodded. 'Oh, I know Katrina.'

'She sort of nagged me into buying a ticket. I wasn't really interested but I thought if . . . well, if you wanted to go with me . . .?'

'Harry, are you . . . are you asking me to go to the disco with you?'

'Er . . . yeah, if you want to?'

125

'I do!' Shannon almost shouted her reply. She knew she ought to at least try to sound a bit calmer. 'Yes, I'd like that very much. I'll get a ticket!'

Jana wanted nothing more than to sleep through the lunch break, but sleep wasn't coming easily.

First she tried the form room, figuring that it was the last place any of her form mates would want to be during a break from lessons. She was right about that, but had forgotten that Mr Jeffries might come in. And he did. Jana was dozing, head resting on her folded arms, when he arrived.

'Jana, are you all right?'

'Oh . . . oh, yes sir,' Jana said sleepily as she sat up.

'I bet you're looking forward to the disco tonight?'

'Oh . . . well . . . not really, sir.'

'No? But I thought all teenagers loved discos.'

Jana could hardly tell the teacher the truth. 'Well, I would come, but . . . but my dad can't afford it, sir.'

'Oh, I see.' Mr Jeffries could be stern and a stickler for the school rules, but he could also be extremely kind. He went to his desk and took out a ticket. 'Here,' he said, giving the ticket to Jana. 'It's a spare.' He smiled. 'Don't tell the Ks!'

'Oh, thank you, sir, but –'

'Think nothing of it,' the teacher said. 'Now go and

get some air. It'll do you a lot more good than dozing in here.'

'Right. Yes. Thank you, sir. Thanks very much.'

Jana didn't go outside for some air. She had another place in mind where she might snatch a few minutes' sleep. On the way she bumped into Shannon, who was heading in the opposite direction. And as they came face to face Shannon threw her arms around Jana and gave her a massive hug.

'Are you OK?' Jana asked, when she was finally released.

'OK!' Shannon beamed. 'OK! Harry Averwood just asked me to the disco! Harry Averwood!'

Before Jana could answer, Shannon was on her way again. 'Got to get a ticket!' she called back as she rushed down the corridor.

The Ks were in the dining hall, counting the ticket sales' cash as Shannon came hurrying up. 'I need a ticket for tonight.'

'We've only got one left,' Kay told her.

Shannon smiled. 'I only need one.'

Kara sneered. 'This morning I heard you say that nothing would make you come to our stupid disco. Changed your mind now?'

Shannon could not stop smiling. 'Yeah, I have, because I got a date.'

The Ks were not impressed. 'Who are you bringing?' Kay said. 'Your dad?'

'No,' Shannon said, completely unruffled by the Ks' sarcasm. 'Harry Averwood.' She picked up her ticket and walked way, with Kara and Kay staring at Katrina.

'Conference!' Kara said and she got up and led her two friends from the dining hall, along the corridor and into the girls' toilets, the place where the Ks frequently held private conversations.

'Katrina, Harry did actually ask you to go with him, didn't he?' Kara asked immediately.

Katrina frowned. 'When I was selling tickets I asked him if he wanted to go to the disco, and he said OK.'

'When you were selling tickets?'

Katrina nodded.

'Right, so all you actually did was sell him a ticket?'

'But that's still no excuse for Shannon to take him off me!'

'Ssshh!' Kara said quickly, before gesturing towards one of the cubicles. They hadn't noticed that the door was closed and, listening closely, they heard the sound of gentle snoring. Kara tiptoed to the next-door cubicle, stood on the lavatory and peered over. Jana was sleeping peacefully.

Kara went back to her friends. 'Smelly girl is sleeping on the toilet,' she whispered.

'That is so gross!' Katrina said.

'Yeah, but it's given us a way to start messing things up for Shannon and Harry. Just play along with what I say.'

Kay and Katrina nodded and then grinned as Kara thumped on the toilet door. Inside the cubicle, Jana woke up with a start and then heard Kara speaking loudly to her friends.

'And dear, sweet-faced Harry Averwood is a love rat, that's what I'm on about!'

Katrina looked blank, but Kay was much quicker to realise where Kara was going. 'Yeah, he asks them out one day and gets rid the next. That's when he's not cheating on them anyway.'

'Exactly,' Kara said as they heard the sounds of movement in the cubicle. She smiled at her friends. 'Poor Shannon, she's got no idea what she's getting herself into.'

'No idea at all,' Kay confirmed.

Katrina was still looking confused.

'If we were close enough to her, we could warn her,' Kara continued. 'But she'd never listen to us. Let's hope one of her friends knows the truth about Harry and cares enough to tell her.'

Kara and Kay smiled and bundled the still bewildered Katrina away. A minute later, once she was sure the coast was clear, Jana emerged from the cubicle and went hunting for Maddy and Rhydian. She quickly blurted out everything she'd heard.

Maddy wasn't convinced that what the Ks had been saying was true and she didn't want to upset Shannon with gossip. But she didn't want Shannon to be hurt again either. 'We'll go to the disco,' Maddy told Rhydian, 'and we'll be there for her if she needs us.'

'Oh, do we really have to?' Rhydian asked, feeling more and more tired as the day wore on.

'We owe her, Rhydian, and she's our friend.'

Rhydian just about stifled a yawn. 'Yeah, all right.'

Seventeen

Jana volunteered to sit in the reception area outside the hall to take coats and tickets for the disco. It suited her perfectly. She could quietly let in Maddy and Rhydian, who were ticketless, and then try to doze once the disco was in full swing. She had no intention of dancing, with Tom or anyone else.

The Ks were bustling about the hall, checking that everything was ready and on the look-out for any last-minute hitches. DJ Darby had just arrived and was sorting through his vast collection of records as the Ks approached.

'Everything OK?' Kara asked.

The DJ shrugged. 'Not too impressed with your PA gear but I guess I'll manage. So if we could just sort out my fee?'

Katrina smiled; she'd been the one who'd booked DJ Darby. 'Yeah, I'll give you the forty quid when we're finished.'

'Forty quid?'

'That's what we agreed.' Katrina looked puzzled. 'Didn't we?'

'No, we did not.' The famous DJ was not happy. 'I remember quite clearly telling you to add another nought when we spoke on the phone last week.'

Katrina turned to Kara and Kay. 'I thought he was joking.'

'I was not joking!'

'But we haven't got four hundred quid.'

The DJ smiled sarcastically. 'Then you haven't got me. Goodnight, ladies.'

While the Ks stood watching, speechless for once, the DJ gathered together his gear and made for the exit, just as Tom came into the room. 'Hey, DJD!' he said, beaming and raising a hand for a high five as the great man approached. But he ignored Tom completely, not even bothering to nod a hello.

Tom shrugged and carried on into the hall, where the Ks were on the stage, clustered around the mixing desk and arguing.

'What's happened?' Tom asked.

Kara stared down at him. 'What does it look like?' she snapped. 'Our star DJ has just walked out on us and we don't have a clue what to do next!'

Tom, carrying his tablet, leapt on to the stage and plugged it into the PA system.

'What are you doing?' Kara said.

'Saving your disco.'

'Can you do it? Really?'

Tom pointed to the tablet. 'Four thousand tracks, two hundred individual playlists, and as for me, there's a small but devoted online following.' He grinned. 'Just stand back and watch.'

The school hall was rocking and Tom was totally in control. Music blared from the speakers and the dance floor was heaving.

Shannon felt fantastic, if a little nervous, as she walked into the room and spotted Harry talking with some of his friends. One of them noticed Shannon. He nudged Harry, who looked up and came hurrying across to his date.

'Shannon, you look great.'

Maddy and Rhydian were among the late arrivals. They both still felt dreadful and would much rather have been tucked up in their beds, but they were there to support Shannon, if she needed them. As they stepped into the reception area they saw Jana fast asleep with her head resting on a pile of coats.

'Seems a shame to wake her,' Rhydian said, grinning. They went into the hall and soon saw Shannon and Harry dancing happily together.

'Still think she needs our support?' Rhydian asked Maddy.

'Rhydian, no one will be happier than me if everything works out for Shannon.'

But Maddy had not noticed the Three Ks whispering together, nor Katrina pass her phone to Kay. The dance floor was packed and it was easy for Kay to squeeze past Harry and slip the phone into his jacket pocket without him noticing.

A couple of minutes later Kay and Kara stepped on to the stage and went over to Tom just as he was lining up the next track.

'We need to cut the music for a minute, Tom,' Kara told him.

'What? But you'll ruin the atmosphere.'

'Just for a minute, it's important.'

She grabbed the mic and the hall went quiet. There were groans from the dance floor.

'Sorry, everyone,' Kara said into the mic, 'just a quick announcement. Katrina's lost her mobile, so could you all be quiet for a minute while we ring it?'

There were more groans, but everyone stayed quiet as Kara called Katrina's number. The phone began to ring instantly and everyone stared at Harry. He reached into his pocket and brought out the ringing mobile.

'It's OK, everyone,' Kay boomed. 'Harry's got it.'

'Yes, she must have left it at his place earlier,' Kara continued with mock innocence as all eyes turned to Shannon and Harry in the middle of the dance floor.

'Shannon,' Harry said, looking completely baffled. 'I don't what they're on about. She never came round to mine, I swear.'

But the humiliation was too much for Shannon. She rushed from the room, her mouth set, her face tense. Maddy raced after her and Harry was about to follow too, but Rhydian barred his way. 'Give her a minute, eh, mate?'

'They set this up,' Harry said, 'they must have. I promise you, I didn't do anything wrong. Look, I really like Shannon, there's no way I'd hurt her.'

Rhydian nodded. Harry seemed totally sincere.

Up on the stage the Ks appeared to be celebrating. Rhydian, instantly suspicious, went over to the stage and whispered a few words to Tom, who glanced over at the Ks.

Kara was still holding the microphone. As the music boomed on, Tom flicked a switch on the desk, which allowed him to listen in through his headphones to what the mic was picking up. And as he listened he smiled and then pressed the *Record* button on the mixing desk.

'Why me?' Shannon said to Maddy as she struggled to put on her coat and ran out into the cold night air.

'Shan!'

'Nothing ever goes right for me. I just wanted one nice thing to happen. Just one . . .'

The double doors to the hall flew back and Jana came bursting out, suddenly wide awake. 'Shannon, you have to hear this! You really have to!"

'If it's some pathetic excuse from Harry. . .!'

'It's not! Come back in, please, you really will want to hear it.'

Jana seemed so certain that Shannon felt she had no option but to go back inside. As she walked back into the hall with Jana and Maddy, they heard Kara and Kay's recorded voices saying the same phrases over and over through the PA system.

'*We did it! Harry and Shannon are so over!*'

'*So over! So over!*'

But Harry and Shannon were not over. As the Ks flounced from the room, Tom brought back the music, but this time it was a slow song. Harry and Shannon moved together and began to dance. And before the song was over, they were sharing their first kiss.

Eighteen

As soon as Liam Hunter learned the location of the camping site for the school orienteering trip was at Aern Hollow he was excited. Aern Hollow was mentioned in his ancestor's journal, the very same ancestor who had shot and killed Maddy's great-great-great-great-uncle William, believing him to be a werewolf.

The tragic shooting had happened over two hundred years previously, but Liam remained as convinced as his ancestor Abraham Hunter had been that werewolves really did exist. And the visit to the ancient woodland was going to give him another chance to prove it. His old relative had left a journal, which pointed the way to an alleged werewolf den – somewhere in Aern Hollow.

Liam was sharing a tent with Jimi and Sam, who were both delighted to be camping out in the wild but far less enthusiastic about listening to their friend reading passages from old Abe's journal just before lights out.

But others nearby were listening with interest, and anxiety. Rhydian was sharing a tent with Tom, while Maddy was in with Shannon and Jana, and all three Wolfbloods had engaged their ultra-sensitive hearing at the first mention of the word *werewolf*.

And Liam's words did not make comfortable listening. Old Abe had been convinced he had found the den and had written out rough directions and made drawings in the journal. And now that he was so close to the spot, Liam was determined to rediscover the den the following day.

The following morning, the class were split into groups for the map-reading exercise.

Rhydian thought they should stay completely clear of anything to do with werewolf den hunts, but Maddy finally convinced him that they had to team up with Liam and his mates so they could divert him from the den – if it did exist.

'William was a member of my pack,' she said determinedly. 'If he did have a den out here, then I want to know about it, and I want to keep Liam away too.'

Tom was chosen as leader of their team, while Jana and Shannon found themselves in a group with the Three Ks, which pleased none of them, especially as Katrina was selected as leader.

The task was to use only a compass and a map to

reach different locations. Mobile phones, with their GPS apps, were not allowed, but each group was given a walkie-talkie in case of emergency.

The groups set off into the woodland. They were each searching for three markers and the first group back with all three markers would be the winners.

Tom's team soon found their first marker. Tom was carrying the map and Jimi held the compass, but Liam was paying more attention to Abe's journal.

'We have to go this way,' he said, pointing in the opposite direction to the way Tom was looking.

'No, it's this way,' Tom told him.

Liam had made up his mind. 'Tom, we're going my way.'

Maddy and Rhydian looked on, saying nothing, while Jimi and Sam just wanted to get on with the race to find the markers.

'Hang on, Liam,' Tom said. 'Jeffries told us not to split up.'

'He wants to go werewolf-den hunting,' Jimi said impatiently.

'Then we'll go with him,' Maddy said quickly. 'If that's all right with you, Tom.'

Tom shrugged his shoulders. 'I guess.'

'We'll catch you up,' Rhydian called as Tom, Jimi and Sam headed off.

'How?' Jimi called back. 'We've got the map.'

'Trust me, we'll find you!'

They were deep in the wood, and although the day was bright the dense tree canopy made the atmosphere dark and gloomy. The only sounds were the occasional burst of birdsong and the tramp of their feet on the leaf litter. As he led the way, Liam was a hundred times more focused than he ever was in the classroom.

'Supposing we find this den?' Maddy asked him, breaking the silence. 'What will you do?'

Liam kept walking and did not look back. 'I dunno. Take photos; phone Doctor Whitewood. You know, the one who came when we found the skeleton. Depends on what we find, I suppose.'

'If we find anything,' Rhydian said.

'You didn't have to come with me.'

'No, I know, I didn't.'

Silence returned and they continued onwards until they reached a barbed wire fence. Attached to it was an old sign that warned that trespassers would be prosecuted.

Rhydian smiled. 'Bad luck, man. Looks like we'll have to go back.'

Liam was already stepping cautiously over the fence.

'You think some sign's gonna stop me? You go back if you're scared.'

He trudged on, regularly glancing down at the journal with its directions and sketches. Maddy and Rhydian reluctantly followed.

After another five minutes, Liam stopped and sighed, glancing all around. 'It says look for two rocks! Like a gateway! I don't understand; they should be here.'

Maddy, hanging back a little, had already spotted the two rocks, which had fallen over and were partially covered with mosses and scrubby bush.

'Go and distract him,' she breathed to Rhydian. 'I'll have a look.'

'Distract him how?'

'Just go!'

Rhydian trudged away and Maddy passed through the gap between the two rocks to an area of flat ground covered with rotting branches and leaf litter. The ground seemed to give a little beneath her feet, but before she could explore further, Liam came hurrying up, with Rhydian in hot pursuit. 'Did you find something?' he demanded urgently. 'Why didn't you call me?'

'I . . . I . . .'

Liam couldn't wait for an answer. 'This is it; it has to be. It's exactly where the journal says the lair is.'

'But there's nothing here.'

'Nothing,' Rhydian repeated. 'I guess your ancestor must have got it wrong.'

'No. There must be a secret entrance or something.' Liam was certain he was in the right place. 'I mean you can't expect them to leave a sign up! The journal says it's here.'

'Look, we've tried,' Rhydian said, 'but we ought to get back to Tom and the others before they go back to base without us.'

He began to manoeuvre Maddy towards the gap in the rocks in the hope that Liam would follow and they could move away from the site, but before they had taken more than a couple of steps there was a sudden terrified yell. They looked back.

Liam had disappeared.

Nineteen

Liam was lying on the ground of the underground den, trapped beneath fallen branches and a larger wooden rafter that had broken away from the wall. The flimsy covering to the den had remained undisturbed for many years but had given way under Liam's weight.

'Liam!' Maddy called as they peered down through a cloud of dust. 'Liam, are you all right?'

'I'm stuck, I can't move. My leg's trapped; and it hurts.' Liam was about two metres down, surrounded by fallen rock and broken wood.

'Hold still! We'll get help!'

Maddy pulled Rhydian back so that Liam wouldn't hear them. 'We should get Jeffries!'

'And I should have my head examined for letting you talk me into this!'

'Yes, all right!'

'I'll go; you stay with him. I'll find our group; they'll be closer than Jeffries.'

'And how will that help?'

'The walkie-talkie; I can call Jeffries.'

A loud groan emerged from the depths of the den. 'I can't move my leg!'

Rhydian hurried away and Maddy went back to the gaping hole. 'Rhydian's gone for help!'

Liam groaned again. 'It's dark down here, throw me a torch.'

Maddy took the torch she was carrying from her jacket pocket. 'Here it comes.'

The torch landed softly on the thickly piled leaf litter and within seconds its beam was flicking around the den. 'This is it!' Liam yelled. 'It must be the werewolf den! There's tunnels and everything.'

'It's probably just badger tunnels.'

'I can see support beams. It's one of those that's on my leg.'

'Maybe it's an old mine, then!'

'No! I'm telling you, this place was made by were-wolves.'

Liam was getting dangerously close to the truth and Maddy knew she had to stop him exploring further. The only way to do that would be by getting him out.

'Can you grab on to something? Pull yourself up?'

Liam, straining with the effort, reached for the closest piece of timber sticking up from the ground. He pulled hard, trying to get upright, but the timber gave way and another fall of wood and stone came crashing down around him.

'Liam!' Maddy screamed.

'You got to get me out!' There was sheer panic in Liam's voice now. 'There's more stuff falling!'

'Stay still!' Maddy yelled. 'I'll look for another entrance!'

She went scrambling away and, using her Wolfblood senses, discovered a much smaller hole, partially hidden in the undergrowth.

'Badger,' Maddy whispered.

Maddy guessed that the badger hole would lead through to the Wolfblood den. But there was no way she could get through the hole in her human form. There was only one way; she had to transform.

Her eyes flashed yellow, the veins in the back of her hands and neck began to pulse and throb, her blood turned silver; the full transformation took less than a minute. Wolf-Maddy sniffed the air and then jumped up and wriggled into the badger hole.

Liam was still unable to move but the dust was beginning to settle and it was easier to see again as the torchlight flicked from wall to wall.

There was a sudden rustling and a scrabbling noise.

Then sniffing. Something was moving, and coming closer.

'Maddy! Maddy, can you hear me?'

In the far wall, Liam could see the opening to a dark, smaller tunnel. The noises were coming from there and getting ever louder.

'Maddy! Maddy, there's something in here! I can hear it! Maddy, it's coming for me! It's a werewolf!'

Panic-stricken, Liam grabbed a fallen piece of rock and hurled it with all his strength at the entrance to the hole. It thudded against the mud and caused another small collapse. But as Liam stared, he clearly saw two yellow eyes and a wolf-like face captured in the beam of the torch he held in trembling fingers.

'Maddy!'

Wolf-Maddy was already backing away, struggling to get clear of the light. The tunnel was wider at this point, wide enough to retransform. It took just seconds and as Maddy regained her human form, she slumped to the mud floor, furious for allowing herself to be seen, even for a moment, in wolf form. But there was nothing she could do about that now, except limit the damage. She had to try to avert complete disaster, so she edged forward through the narrow gap and pulled herself into the den.

The torchlight flicked over her face and she squeezed her eyes shut and turned her head away.

'Maddy! Maddy, it's you!'

'Of course it's me. Take the torch off me!'

'Did you see it?'

Maddy's heart was thumping, but she knew she had to stay calm as she got to her feet. 'See what?'

'The werewolf! It was right there, where you are now!'

'I didn't see a thing. Must have been a badger!'

She crept forward, moving carefully so as not to disturb any more of the support beams.

'No, but think about it, Maddy! That beast Shannon was on about for so long, no one ever found it. Then the bones we found were stolen. It's werewolves, it has to be!'

Maddy looked down at the wooden beam, trying to work out if she could lift it. 'You're being daft. It must have been kids who stole the bones.'

'Why would they? The werewolf exists, and this is where it lives!'

'There has to be another explanation,' Maddy said, attempting to be dismissive.

'There's a werewolf! Why won't you accept it? It's almost like you're trying to protect it. And . . . and how did you get down here?'

'Through a badger hole. I heard you shouting.'

'You? Through a badger hole? That doesn't make sense.'

'Just be quiet and hold still, will you,' Maddy said, reaching for the beam. 'I'm gonna try and lift this off.'

Maddy heaved at the beam, lifting it a little. 'Quick, Liam! Quick!'

Liam groaned in pain as he rolled to one side. Maddy could not take the weight for long. She let go and as it thudded back down on to the earth Liam tried to clamber to his feet. But the pain was too much. He staggered backwards against the mud wall, knocking away a smaller beam.

'Liam, stay still! You'll bring the whole roof down on us!'

Maddy's shouted warning was too late. With a thunderous roar, another load of dry earth came tumbling downwards.

Rhydian reached Tom and the others far quicker than any human would have managed. In seconds he was on the walkie-talkie, explaining to Mr Jeffries what had happened and giving directions to the site.

Mr Jeffries set off for the site, having told all the other groups that the emergency situation meant they must abandon their task and return to the base camp.

'Can you get these three back?' Jana said quietly to Shannon after they heard the message.

148

Shannon nodded. 'I think so. Where are you going?'

'To help Maddy.'

She hurtled away, not running at Wolfblood speed until she was certain she was out of sight of the others.

Rhydian was on his way back to the den too. The two Wolfbloods raced through the woodland at breakneck speed, dodging trees, ignoring the brambles and bushes, as they raced towards their friend. They met up before reaching the site of the ancient den, but when they arrived there was nothing to be seen but a cloud of dust rising vertically into the air.

'Maddy!' Rhydian yelled, close to panic. 'Maddy!'

For a moment, nothing moved, but then earth around them seemed to shift and sway and a second hole appeared in the little clearing.

Earth was already tumbling inwards as Maddy's hand emerged from the hole. Rhydian and Jana dived and grabbed her, quickly pulling her clear. And then they were all scrabbling for Liam, pulling him to safety as the earth around them gave way.

By the time, Mr Jeffries arrived the three Wolfbloods and the injured Liam were on the move. Liam, limping slowly along, had one arm draped over Rhydian's shoulder and was being supported on the other side by Jana.

'Liam, are you all right?' Mr Jeffries asked anxiously.

'Don't think it's broken, sir.'

'But what were you doing here? I told you all to stick together.'

'My fault, sir,' Liam admitted. 'I was exploring and I got lost. These three came looking for me.'

Mr Jeffries looked from Maddy, to Rhydian, to Jana. 'And what are *you* doing here?' he said to Jana. 'You're in another group completely.'

'I heard you on the talkie thingy, sir. I thought you'd need help.'

'But . . . how did you get here so quickly?'

'I ran.'

Mr Jeffries turned to Rhydian. 'And how about you?'

'I ran too, sir.'

'You . . . you ran . . . But . . .' Mr Jeffries shook his head, completely mystified.

Back at the camp they were taking down the tents at the end of an eventful expedition. Everyone was working, with the exception of Liam, who sat on a canvas chair with his injured leg resting on a stool. His eyes were fixed on Maddy.

'So, you reckon you saw a werewolf?' Sam asked the question, his voice heavy with sarcasm.

'Yep,' Liam answered simply.

'And did Maddy see this werewolf?' Jimi asked, folding a tent pole.

'No. That's what's weird. Really weird.'

'Yeah, well maybe Maddy didn't see it because it wasn't there.'

Liam didn't even look at his friends. His eyes were still on Maddy, who was working with her friends, and only too well aware that her every move was being watched.

'I know what I saw,' Liam said, 'and she was in the exact spot. She *had* to have seen it, too . . . unless . . .'

Jimi and Sam looked at their friend.

'Unless what?' Jimi asked.

Liam spoke softly and deliberately, as though the truth was slowly dawning. 'Unless *she's* the werewolf.'

Sam laughed. 'You sure you didn't get a crack on the head?'

Jimi was laughing, too. 'Maddy Smith: a werewolf. Seriously, man, you must be concussed.'

'Laugh all you want,' Liam said quietly, 'but I know what I know. And it all fits together now. It all makes sense.'

Twenty

Parents' evening was not an event that most students at Bradlington High School looked forward to.

There were too many potentially unpleasant surprises as parents trooped from one teacher to another, expecting and hoping to hear the best about their child but sometimes hearing the worst.

And parents' evening was even more of a problem if there was no parent around to hear what the teachers had to say, which was exactly the situation Jana was facing. With the help of Maddy, Rhydian, Tom and Shannon, Jana was giving the battered old caravan that she'd made her home a spring clean, something she would never have dreamed of doing when she lived as part of the wild pack. But Jana had changed a great deal, and was enjoying her new way of life in the human world more and more.

Parents' evening was going to be a problem though, and the friends were discussing what to do about it when Rhydian suddenly stopped working and sniffed the air.

Maddy and then Jana did exactly the same thing. The Wolfbloods' heightened sense of smell had recognised one of their own.

And Rhydian knew exactly who it was. 'Mum.'

Ceri was standing a little distance from them, watching and waiting. Rhydian rushed over to his mother and they hugged.

'How are you, my beautiful boy?'

'I'm good, and it's great to see you, but what are you doing here? Is Alric . . .?'

Ceri raised a hand. 'Wait.'

She walked across to the caravan and went directly to Jana, and for a moment, the others feared the encounter might explode into violence.

But then Ceri dropped to one knee and bowed her head. She spoke softly and humbly. 'Your father has been exiled. You are the new alpha, the leader of our pack.'

Jana's jaw dropped as Ceri spoke, but as the words sunk in, her first thoughts were still for Alric, even though he'd disowned and banished her. 'Is my father hurt?'

Ceri shook her wild tangle of dark hair. 'Nothing is wounded but his pride.'

'Then what happened?'

'He . . . he lost his mind. But your priority is to the pack now. This is your birthright; your destiny.'

'But I can't just leave my father, I should find him.'

'No. A good leader puts their pack first, your father forgot that.' She got to her feet and looked at Rhydian, who had joined them. 'All your father thought about was destroying my son.'

'I . . . I need to think,' Jana muttered.

Rhydian and his mother watched as Jana walked away, deep in thought.

'It's a bit much for a kid, isn't it, Mum?' Rhydian said. 'Pack leader?'

'Her father raised her for this,' Ceri replied. 'She'll do what is right. And you can return home too.'

'Whoa,' Rhydian said, raising both hands. 'It's not as simple as that any more.'

'You will be alpha male to her female,' Ceri continued as though Rhydian had not spoken.

Jana paced up and down, her mind in turmoil. She needed help and advice, and the person she turned to was Maddy. 'What do I do?' she asked. 'My life is here now.'

'Then stay,' Maddy replied simply.

'But if the pack destroys itself, then their blood is on my hands. I have to go.' Jana seemed to be answering her own question. 'The pack will expect me to rule by fear, that's our history, and they hate change. But I can't rule by fear.'

'So what will you do?'

Jana considered for a moment. 'I must change our ways.' She nodded towards Ceri. 'And I'd better start now.'

Jana, accompanied by her friends, went back to Rhydian and Ceri.

'I'll return as leader,' Jana said simply.

Ceri bowed her head as a sign of acknowledgement.

'On one condition,' Jana added. 'The pack must change.'

Ceri looked up, her eyes flashing. 'Change?'

Slowly and thoughtfully, Jana explained how she would never want to destroy the wild Wolfblood culture but that she believed to survive in the modern world, the pack needed to learn to trust and have contact with tame Wolfbloods, and even humans.

But the softly spoken words seemed to confuse Ceri; Jana's ideas were alien to everything she had ever known.

'The pack respect you as an elder,' Jana went on. 'If you back me on this, *they'll* respect my decisions too.'

'I will do as you order,' Ceri said surprisingly meekly.

'I don't need your submission,' Jana said with a shake of her head, 'I need your support.'

'Then I will support you.'

Jana smiled. 'Good. Then until we leave you will live

life as a human. Here. And tomorrow night, you will come to the school parents' evening.'

'What?' Rhydian said, before anyone else had a chance to speak.

'I need someone, a parent,' Jana told him. 'Who better than Ceri?'

'But you can't ask my mum to do this,' Rhydian said. 'The school will be full of people.'

'And she might wolf out,' Maddy added.

'That's what you said about me,' Jana said. She looked from one friend to another. 'Will you help me on this?'

One after another, her friends nodded.

'What do you need us to do?' Maddy asked.

Daniel and Emma were far from pleased when they heard about their part in the plan, but the safety of their pack was always their first priority, so they agreed to Maddy's suggestion of a meeting at their house.

The Wolfbloods were sitting around the dining table, where discussions were taking place over a meal. Maddy had insisted Tom and Shannon be there too, as they were now also members of her pack. Sharing a meal had seemed like a good idea to Emma, but she was having second thoughts as she watched Ceri rip apart and devour a large hunk of raw meat.

'Let's talk about parents' evening,' Maddy said brightly, attempting to draw attention away from Ceri's unusual table manners.

Emma's eyes were still on Ceri. 'So, do you think you can recognise when the wolf is close to the surface?'

'I'll look after her,' Jana said quickly.

'But it'll be totally different to everything she knows. She won't cope.'

'Mum can do this,' Rhydian said defensively.

'And what if she can't?'

Jana's eyes flashed. 'I told you, I'll look after her!'

'But it makes no difference to you!' Emma responded angrily. 'You're leaving anyway!'

Suddenly, as Tom and Shannon watched in amazement, all the Wolfbloods but Maddy were on their feet, snarling, growling, eyes flashing, veins pulsing.

'Stop it!' Maddy yelled. 'Stop it, all of you!'

Slowly, the Wolfbloods regained their composure and sat down, but the atmosphere was still tense.

'It doesn't seem as though there's much point in us being here,' Jana snarled to Emma.

'Oh no!' Maddy snapped. 'This was your idea, Jana, and we all agreed to help. So let's get on with it!'

So they did, although the Smiths were unable to disguise their doubts about the plan. But they reluctantly

157

agreed to help at the parents' event the following evening.

And after some gentle persuasion from Maddy, they also agreed to allow Ceri to spend the night in their den. It wasn't the wilderness, which Ceri would have preferred, but at least the stone ledges, mud floor and wooden branches made her feel more at home than sat at the table upstairs.

She was prowling around, trying to familiarise herself with the space, while Jana and Rhydian stood watching.

'I let you down earlier,' Jana told her, 'losing my temper like that.'

Ceri was much more interested in blaming the Smiths. 'You see what the tame ones are like. We should leave now, the three of us.'

'No,' Jana said firmly. 'You must make your peace with them, like I have. Learn to understand their ways.'

Ceri sighed and nodded.

'I must leave now, with Tom and Shannon,' Jana continued. 'So I'll see you tomorrow.'

When they were alone, Ceri spoke quietly to her son. 'Jana is no leader; she is still a cub.'

'What?' Rhydian said, surprised. 'Then why are you here?'

'You think I do all this for her?'

'Well, don't you?'

'She won't be strong enough on her own, even with

my help. And without you there too, Aran and Meinir will take over and then you'll never be allowed to see me again. *You* are the reason I'm doing this, Rhydian. You must come back to the wild. You must!'

Upstairs, with Ceri off the scene, the mood was much calmer. While Tom and Shannon were saying their good-nights to Emma and Maddy, Daniel took the chance of a quiet word with Jana. He was the leader of his pack and Jana was to be leader of hers, so they now had much in common. And Daniel wanted to know why it was so important for Jana to take Ceri to the school, when they were both going to leave anyway.

Jana's reply proved that she was already maturing into her new role. 'I want the pack to change,' she said thoughtfully. 'Ceri needs to understand what I've been doing and how I've changed. Meeting the teachers and the other pupils will help her do that. Then she can help me when we return to the wild.'

Daniel nodded. 'It's a risky strategy.'

'I know,' Jana said. 'But if things are ever going to change then it's a risk I have to take.'

Twenty-one

The long night alone in the caravan with only her own thoughts for company did nothing to boost Jana's confidence, and her brave and courageous attitude seemed to have deserted her the following day at school.

She was quiet and unusually hesitant during the first lesson and full of self-doubt when she spoke to Maddy at break time. 'I'm not sure who I am any more. Wild Wolfblood? Tame? Human?'

Maddy realised that Jana's departure was likely to see Rhydian leaving too. It was the worst possible scenario for her, but even so, she wanted to help her Wolfblood friend. 'You're all of those things, Jana, and more. You're a survivor and you know both worlds and that's what sets you apart.'

Jana smiled, grateful for Maddy's words, but the doubts remained. Truth and being truthful had become vital to her over the past few weeks, but there was one truth she had kept from Maddy. Now she knew it was time to tell all. 'There's something you have to know, Maddy,' she said. 'I wasn't banished when I first came here. My father sent me, to bring Rhydian back for punishment. I was meant to tempt him back to the pack. But I couldn't do it because I fell in love . . .'

Maddy's eyes widened. This was a truth she really did not want to hear.

'. . . with the human world,' Jana continued.

Maddy breathed a sigh of relief. 'So . . . that's why Alric came back?'

Jana nodded. 'I fooled you then, and now I'm fooling myself. I have to stop this; I can't let Ceri come to the parents' evening.'

'You can and you must,' Maddy said. 'If you call it off you'll lose Ceri's respect and you need her on your side if you're ever going to win over your pack.'

Jana sighed; she knew Maddy was right.

Jana spent the hours between the end of school and the evening event back at the caravan, getting her thoughts in order and planning her strategy. The prospect of not just returning to the wild but returning as pack leader was daunting. She was having to grow up fast.

She was the first of the Wolfbloods to arrive for

parents' evening and when Rhydian arrived with his own foster mum, Mrs Vaughan, Jana managed to grab a quick word with him. 'I want you to promise me something,' she said.

'What?'

'You know that when I leave, I want you to come too.'

'Of course I know.'

'But more than that, I want you to follow your heart, do what you really want to do. It's my pack now, not my father's, or your mother's.'

Rhydian smiled. 'Thanks, Jana.'

Maddy and her parents were just arriving, so Rhydian headed back to Mrs Vaughan. He was booked to be first in to see their form teacher and head of year, Mr Jeffries.

Jana smiled her approval as she caught sight of Ceri. She had been given a serious makeover by Emma, who had dressed the wild Wolfblood in some of her own clothes.

'You look good,' Jana said. 'Just remember, you're my mum.'

Ceri was hardly listening. Her eyes were on Rhydian, who was chatting with Mrs Vaughan as they waited to see Mr Jeffries.

'That's her, isn't it?' Ceri said, gesturing towards Mrs Vaughan. 'Rhydian's human mother.'

'Foster mother,' Maddy said before Jana could reply. 'That's a human who loves and supports someone else's cub because it's the right thing to do.' She nodded towards Jana. 'It's a bit like you and Jana. She might be your new leader, but you're the grown up and you'll do what's best for her.'

Ceri watched Rhydian and his foster mother chatting happily. 'She loves him.'

'Enough to make him feel safe, anyway,' Maddy replied.

Jana slipped an arm through Ceri's and smiled. 'Here we go, then. Just stick with me, *Mum,* and you'll be fine.'

Rhydian squirmed in his seat as he listened to Mr Jeffries.

'I'm afraid that despite my best efforts these behavioural issues are still a problem.'

Mrs Vaughan listened patiently but was determined to be supportive of her foster son. 'We know, and we're trying to work on it.'

'But,' Mr Jeffries continued, and this time his voice sounded more positive, 'he's an incredibly gifted young man in sport, and in art, but I do wish he'd be more of a team player. He's got great potential, but he needs to choose which way he wants to go.'

Rhydian almost smiled at the irony of his teacher's words. He was right; there was a vitally important choice to be made. 'You don't need to worry, sir,' he said. 'It won't be a problem any more.'

Mr Jeffries raised his eyebrows. 'Well, I'm glad to hear you sounding so confident about the future, Rhydian.'

'Oh, I am, sir.'

As Rhydian and his foster mother got up to move on to their next appointment, Jana was carefully guiding Ceri around the school while she explained how her human side had become such an important part of her life.

'Keep calm here,' she said soothingly, as they made their way along a crowded corridor. 'In geography and science I've been learning about the wilderness; why it's shrinking and how humans mess it up. I've learned a lot about humans, how they mess things up but mainly try to learn from their mistakes. It's called human nature.'

Ceri was listening intently, taking in everything Jana was telling her, learning about this strange new world. It was going better than Jana could have dreamed of when suddenly a woman walking in the other direction accidentally bumped into Ceri. The woman barely glanced back as she continued with a quick, 'Sorry.' But Ceri spun around; hers eyes blazing yellow.

'Ceri!' Jana warned as her *mum* fought to stop from wolfing out.

'In here,' Jana said, bundling Ceri into the girls' toilets and over to the row of sinks. She turned on a tap. 'Splash cold water on your face, it helps.' But Ceri was mesmerised by her reflection in the mirror, something she had rarely seen, and never dressed as she was like a human.

She reached up with one hand and touched her reflection. The action seemed to calm her completely, which was extremely fortunate because at that moment, the Three Ks walked in.

Katrina was upset and tearful. 'They hate me!' she moaned. 'Every single teacher in the entire school hates me!'

'They don't hate you,' Kara said, trying to pacify her friend. 'It's just your work they're not keen on.'

Katrina was barely listening. 'And now I'm grounded for weeks!'

The Ks suddenly noticed Ceri, who was staring at

them, inhaling as she smelled their exotic array of perfumes.

Katrina and Kay stared back, looking hostile, but Kara was doing her best to create a good impression at parents' evening. 'Hello,' she said, smiling at Ceri, 'you must be Jana's mum. I'm Kara, student representative on the school council.'

She held out her right hand to shake hands, but Ceri had never experienced such a gesture. But she wanted to do the right thing for Jana, so she held out her hand too, touching the tips of Kara's fingers with hers. Kara looked blank for a moment but then clasped Ceri's outstretched hand in hers and shook it once before quickly letting go.

'So, not a good night, then?' Jana said to Katrina, looking to bring an end to the awkward moment.

Katrina was still tearful, so Kara answered for them both. 'It's not her fault, it's the teachers.'

'I do try,' Katrina almost wailed. 'But they don't take me seriously.'

'But they will if Kara and Kay help you,' Jana said kindly. 'You three always stick together, no matter what. So prove the teachers wrong.'

'And how are we meant to do that?' Kara asked.

'By you and Kay helping Katrina with what you're good at.'

Kara thought for a moment. 'She's right,' she said to Kay. 'I can help Katrina with science and you can help with maths. We'll show those teachers.'

'Yeah,' Kay said defiantly. 'We're the Ks. Mess with one of us and they mess with us all.'

Katrina wiped away her tears and smiled. 'Thanks, Jana,' she beamed.

'No worries,' Jana said and the Ks went strutting away.

'They listened to you,' Ceri said to Jana as they emerged into the corridor.

Jana smiled. 'Well, don't sound so surprised. Hold out your hand.'

Ceri did as instructed and was practising the correct way to shake hands when Maddy and her parents came down the corridor.

'How's it going?' Daniel asked.

'Good,' Jana replied, smiling. 'Really good.' But her smile faded as Rhydian and Mrs Vaughan approached. There was no way of avoiding a meeting between Ceri and Rhydian's foster mum now.

'Hi, everyone,' Rhydian said slightly nervously.

Maddy and her family knew Mrs Vaughan well and said their hellos, but then it was Jana and Ceri's turn.

'This is my friend, Jana,' Rhydian said to Mrs Vaughan. 'And her mum, Ceri.'

Mrs Vaughan held out her hand to Ceri. 'Lovely to meet you.'

Everyone watched anxiously as Ceri hesitated. But then she smiled, reached out and took Mrs Vaughan's hand in hers and shook it warmly.

'You're . . . you're doing a good job,' she said. 'With Rhydian.'

Mrs Vaughan looked surprised, but far from displeased at the unexpected compliment. 'Thank you.'

'Time for us to see Mr Jeffries, Mum,' Jana said, guiding Ceri quickly away. The brief encounter with Mrs Vaughan had been a welcome bonus, but the toughest test of the evening was still to come in the one-to-one meeting with Jana's form teacher.

As Jana and Ceri went into the classroom and the door closed, Maddy and her parents, along with Rhydian, could not resist loitering close by and engaging their Wolfblood hearing to eavesdrop on exactly what was being said.

They heard the usual introductions and a short summary from Mr Jeffries detailing Jana's efforts in the classroom to date. And then he went on to give his own thoughts. 'So apart from natural sciences, I'd be lying if I told you Jana was our most gifted academic student. But we've found that she has a remarkable, instinctive intelligence.

She's fantastic at sport, fiercely competitive, and she's a natural leader and helper of others. She was fearless and rushed to help when there was an incident on our recent camping trip,' Mr Jeffries continued. 'Yes, I can say quite categorically, that if I was ever in danger or trouble, this is one lady I'd want by my side.'

Jana glanced across to Ceri, who was smiling proudly.

They met up again in the corridor a little later: Maddy and her parents, Jana and Ceri, and Rhydian.

'So, did Ceri pass your test?' Maddy asked Jana.

'She did,' Jana said, 'and that's why she's staying in the caravan with me tonight. We're leaving at first light.'

Jana and Ceri turned to Rhydian, both wanting to know whether he would be with them on their departure for the wilderness.

'I . . . I have to go.' He gestured towards Mrs Vaughan, who was waiting near the exit doors. 'I'll see you in the morning.'

He hurried away and as Jana and Maddy walked down the corridor, Jana put an arm around Maddy's waist. 'One pack leader to another,' she said quietly. 'Whatever he decides, no hard feelings, eh?'

Maddy nodded. 'No hard feelings.'

They went to say their goodbyes to Tom and Shannon while Daniel and Emma waited outside with Ceri.

'So,' Emma said to Ceri, 'you passed Jana's test. Did she pass yours?'

Ceri nodded slowly. 'She will make a great pack leader.'

Twenty-two

Dawn had broken and Ceri was standing close to the caravan in the stillness of morning as Rhydian approached with a rucksack slung over one shoulder.

But Ceri was not fooled by her son's prompt arrival or by the rucksack he carried. She knew what he was going to say before the words left his mouth.

'The thing is, Mum . . .'

'You were never really wild, my beautiful boy.'

Rhydian smiled and took his mum's hands in his. 'You will look after Jana, won't you?'

'I will be her rock,' Ceri said proudly. 'Her . . . foster mother.'

'And I'll come and visit. Two packs, two families; it'll be the best of both worlds.'

It wasn't the outcome Ceri had wished for but she was determined now to respect her son's decision. 'And I will always be there for you.'

Jana had heard their voices. She emerged from the caravan, ready to travel, and it was the look on her face that said she too had guessed that Rhydian had made the decision to stay. 'I'll miss you,' she said softly.

'Any way I can help you, I will,' Rhydian told her gently and sincerely. 'But I belong here now.'

Jana nodded sadly but smiled as Rhydian bowed his head to her, acknowledging that she was now the true leader of the wild Wolfblood pack.

As the three Wolfbloods stood together, there were footsteps and Maddy, Tom and Shannon came hurrying into the clearing.

'We couldn't let you go without seeing you off,' Maddy said.

'And I want to give this to you, Mum,' Rhydian said, undoing the rucksack. He took out a sketchbook and watched as Ceri proudly turned the pages filled with his drawings. There were portraits of his friends and some of his landscapes. Ceri studied each page carefully.

'They're so good,' she breathed.

'Look at the last page,' Rhydian said.

Ceri turned to the final page, where there was a drawing of a wolf and a young cub. It was the perfect likeness of Ceri and Rhydian's half-brother, Bryn, in their wolf form.

'Tell Bryn I love him too, yeah?' Rhydian said.

Tears filled Ceri's eyes as she hugged her son.

Maddy went to hug Jana. 'We'll tell Jeffries your family moved on,' she said. 'And we don't know where.'

The morning sun was beginning to pierce the trees. It was time to go.

'I love you guys,' Jana simply.

There were no goodbyes; it was not an ending. Maddy and her friends watched Jana and Ceri walk to the tree line before pausing to look back.

And then, like shadows, they were gone.

Twenty-three

It was somehow inevitable that Alric would return to seek vengeance and it happened on the day of the next full moon. Maddy and Rhydian had met up to travel to school together and then suddenly they were running for their lives through thick woodland.

Alric had taken them completely by surprise, grabbing furiously at Rhydian, who just managed to evade his clutches and hurtle away at Wolfblood speed with Maddy at his side.

The shamed wild Wolfblood no longer had anything to lose. His conniving and trickery had led him to lose the respect of his daughter and since then he had been stripped of the leadership of his pack and banished. He had nothing, he was alone, without pride or honour, and in his troubled and unbalanced mind it was all the fault of Rhydian.

They were running at lightning-fast speed, dodging past trees and bushes, ignoring spiky brambles and thorns. Maddy and Rhydian knew the landscape better than their pursuer and after a frantic chase, appeared temporarily at least to have shaken him off.

Rhydian crouched down and let the fingers of one hand touch the ground as he entered the state Wolfbloods call Eolas, which his mother had taught him. It enabled him to feel and sense even more than his normal heightened Wolfblood senses. He was in tune with the earth and nature and soon could visualise in his mind where Alric lurked.

But Alric was using also Eolas to hunt them down. Rhydian clearly 'saw' the wild Wolfblood visualising their whereabouts and then start to run towards them.

Before Rhydian could get to his feet, Maddy's mobile began to ring. Rhydian instantly clutched both hands to the sides of his head and rolled on the ground. The signals and waves of electricity generated by the phone were clashing with Eolas, causing his head to buzz and jangle with pain. Maddy switched off the phone and pulled Rhydian to his feet.

'Rhydian, I've got an idea!'

'We have to run, now!' Rhydian gasped.

They ran, but this time not blindly. Maddy was deliberately leading their pursuer to a specific location. She skidded to a halt and pulled Rhydian to a standstill at her side.

'Wait!' she yelled.

The wait was not long. After a few moments the demented figure of Alric loomed into view. He saw them and stopped running, his face wild with rage.

'No humans to hide you this time,' he snarled.

'What do you want, Alric?' Maddy demanded bravely.

'I want my pack! I want my daughter! But as I cannot have either I will have the one who took them from me!' He pointed his arm and a long accusing finger at Rhydian. 'Him!'

'Well, you can't have him, because my pack will be here any second!'

'What's that to me?'

Maddy chose her next words very deliberately. 'And Jana's with them!'

Rhydian turned to stare quizzically at Maddy as Alric froze. 'Jana,' the older Wolfblood breathed. 'But she can't be.'

He looked around but saw nothing. Then he crouched down and touched his fingers to the earth, entering the Eolas state to try to visualise the whereabouts of his daughter.

It was exactly what Maddy had hoped he would do. After a few seconds, Alric let out a terrible roar of pain and fell to the ground, clutching at his head and moaning.

As Rhydian looked on in confusion, Maddy grabbed his arm and pointed upwards. 'Electricity pylons,' she said, 'they mess with Eolas. This is our chance; let's go!'

As Alric squirmed on the ground, Maddy and Rhydian hurtled away, knowing for certain it would be some time before their hunter would be in any condition to follow.

Liam had returned to school for the first time after his brush with disaster in the Wolfblood den. His leg had mended but his face still wore reminders of the terrifying experience. And it also wore something new – a look of grim determination. Liam believed beyond any doubt that he had seen a werewolf while trapped in what he thought was its lair, and nothing could shake that belief, not even the scorn of his best friends Sam and Jimi.

The class had arrived at school that morning prepared for their English presentations, with everyone due to talk on a topic of their choice. But there was no sign of Maddy or Rhydian. Tom called their mobiles but received no answer.

'Where are they?' he whispered to Shannon as they listened to the first presentation.

Shannon shrugged. 'It's full moon tonight, maybe they're letting off steam.'

Liam had plans of his own for the night of the full moon. 'I'm going down into those tunnels tonight,' he said quietly to Jimi and Sam, 'and I'm gonna catch myself a werewolf.'

'You're crazy,' Jimi answered. 'The only reason you got out last time was because Maddy Smith was there to save you.'

'Yeah, well, I'm not sure about Maddy Smith. The werewolf must have run straight past her, so how come she didn't see it?'

'Cos she's not crazy, Liam,' Sam offered.

Miss Fitzgerald was running the session. She stood up and gestured to the speaker to pause. 'Boys! Will you please keep quiet and give our speakers the respect they deserve.'

The talk continued but Liam was soon muttering again. 'There's a werewolf in those tunnels; I saw it. And I'm giving you two a chance to share in the glory of finding it with me.'

Kara was the next speaker. Her presentation was called, 'Make-up: Can it Make Anyone Fabulous?' and she chose Shannon as her demonstration model – much to Shannon's horror! But she was bravely enduring the torment of being excessively made up when the doors to the hall swung open and Maddy and Rhydian came in, both looking as though they had been dragged through a hedge.

'Oh, it's nice of you to turn up,' Miss Fitzgerald called from the stage. 'Sit down, please. But don't get too comfortable, Rhydian, you're up next.'

Kara's talk finally came to an end, and while she gathered together her many powders, pots and lipglosses and Shannon cleansed her face, Tom took the chance to snatch a few words with Maddy and Rhydian.

'So what happened to you two?'

'Alric,' Rhydian answered.

'What?'

'He ambushed us on the way here.'

'But . . . but you've lost him, right?'

'For now,' Maddy whispered.

The stage was clear and Miss Fitzgerald was ready to get on. 'Right, Rhydian, we're ready for you.'

Rhydian sighed, climbed reluctantly on to the stage and muttered the title of his presentation, which he had hastily prepared the previous evening. 'Being in Foster Care.'

'Louder please, Rhydian,' Miss Fitzgerald boomed. 'We want everyone at the back to hear, don't we?'

'*Being in Foster Care!*'

'Thank you.'

Rhydian stumbled and stuttered his way into the talk, but his mind was totally elsewhere. As he spoke his eyes constantly flicked towards the door and windows. Alric was out there somewhere and Rhydian knew only too well that Alric did not give up a hunt easily, if at all.

But he was saved from his discomfort, and so were his classmates, when the bell for break time sounded. Rhydian jumped from the stage and headed off with Maddy, Tom and Shannon to the sanctuary of the photographic darkroom, where they could talk privately.

Outside, on the edge of the playground, Jimi, Sam and Liam, were taking part in a half-hearted football kick around with a few other boys.

But Liam was still attempting to get his mates to accompany him on his trip to the werewolf lair. 'So are you scared to come with me, then?' he asked as the ball was kicked away.

'Why would we be scared of imaginary animals?' Sam said.

'Or maybe you're just scared of the dark? Or mud? Or worms?'

Liam's deliberate taunts were more than Jimi's fragile ego could take. 'We're *not* scared!'

'Then come with me!'

Jimi and Sam exchanged a look.

'Fine!' Jimi said. 'We'll go werewolf hunting with you!'

Liam grinned, unaware of the wild-looking man approaching swiftly across the playing fields. Within seconds he was looming over him.

'Boy.'

Liam turned and almost staggered back as he saw the strange and menacing man.

'Where is Rhydian?' Alric demanded.

'I . . . I dunno,' Liam said, baffled.

The stranger turned and stalked across the playground to where the Three Ks were chatting.

'Girl, where is Rhydian?' he said to Kay.

The Ks, unlike Liam just seconds earlier, were completely unruffled. Their minds were still on Kara's comprehensive make-up presentation.

'I think he went to the darkroom,' Kay answered, pointing nonchalantly towards the school buildings. 'Over there.'

Alric marched away.

'And a "thank you" wouldn't kill you,' Kay called as he went.

The wild Wolfblood had been into the school building once before. On the previous occasion he had hesitated before passing through the doors, but not this time. He swept in and climbed the staircase, taking two steps at a time.

At the top he paused, sniffed the air, then strode down the corridor, just as Mr Jeffries came from his form room.

'Er . . . excuse me,' the teacher asked, 'can I help you?'

The wild Wolfblood glared. 'Where is the darkroom?'

'And . . . who exactly are you?'

Alric's eyes narrowed. 'Where is Rhydian?'

Mr Jeffries was not the biggest of men, but he was no coward and he was not going to be intimidated. 'I'm going to have to ask you to leave now.'

Further down the corridor a door opened and Rhydian and Maddy emerged. They had picked up Alric's scent and knew they had to get out of the building quickly.

'Now I have him!' Alric growled.

He went to charge forward as Rhydian and Maddy dashed away, but Mr Jeffries bravely grabbed the wild Wolfblood's arm and clung on tightly. With a vicious snarl, Alric swung around and pushed the teacher against the wall, pinning him there for a moment and glaring into his eyes before charging away. As Mr Jeffries got on the phone to the police and Tom rang Maddy's parents, Maddy and Rhydian were hurtling across the playing field, Alric in pursuit.

Twenty-four

Maddy and Rhydian had reached the woods but knew that just running aimlessly was hopeless. Alric was strong and fit and an expert hunter; he would track them down eventually. They had to throw him off their scent.

'The river,' Maddy said as they paused to catch their breath, 'we'll split up and meet at the river.'

She ran off in one direction and Rhydian took another as they attempted to confuse their relentless pursuer. After a few minutes, they were together again, standing on a ledge above the river.

'He'll lose our scent once we're in the water,' Maddy said.

They held hands and jumped, splashing down into the swiftly flowing woodland river. The water was not deep but it was freezing. They waded together upstream for a short distance.

Clambering up the far bank, and soaked through and shivering, they moved on, finally coming to a halt in a small copse.

'Think we've lost him.' Rhydian said, panting.

'Told you we would.'

Rhydian managed a smile before sinking to his knees, then flopping to the ground and rolling over on to his back to stare at the sky.

Maddy was about to do exactly the same thing, when there was a shriek of triumph and Alric dropped from a tree and grabbed her around the waist.

'Maddy!' Rhydian screamed, leaping to his feet.

Maddy struggled but Alric was too strong, wrapping both arms around her and lifting her.

'Alric, please. . .!' Rhydian begged.

'I've lost everything!' he snarled. 'Now it's your turn!'

'But it's me you want! I'm here! I give up; do what you want with me! But let Maddy go, please!'

'Why?' the wild Wolfblood howled. 'Why should I show this one mercy? What mercy did you show my daughter?'

'Rhydian saved your daughter,' Maddy yelled and she fought to break free. '*You* abandoned her, Alric! You!'

Alric almost exploded in fury as he dropped Maddy and raised a clawed hand to hit her.

But Maddy stood her ground defiantly. Alric hesitated, staring blankly at the courageous young girl who refused to cower and submit to his fury. And then in his confused and bewildered state, he suddenly believed he could see Jana and not Maddy bravely facing up to him.

'Jana,' he whispered. He lowered his hand, and suddenly all the fight and fury seemed to drain from him.

Maddy backed slowly away, joining Rhydian. As they watched the wild Wolfblood sink to his knees in utter despair, Emma and Daniel came racing through the trees.

'Mam.'

'Maddy, are you . . .?'

'We're all right, Mam.'

Daniel and Emma instinctively moved to put themselves between the young members of their pack and the wild Wolfblood. But there was no wildness now. Alric simply stared ahead, as the realisation that he was responsible for his own downfall finally hit home.

'What did you say to him?' Emma asked.

'Just . . . just told him the truth,' Maddy said.

The police officer was taking notes but it was obvious from what Maddy and Rhydian were saying that his enquiry would go no further. They had returned to school with Daniel and Emma, having prepared their story on the way.

'Jana's a former pupil,' Mr Jeffries said to the police officer. 'A traveller family.'

'And Jana's dad blamed me for her leaving,' Rhydian added.

This was news to his form teacher. 'You? But why?'

'They were close,' Emma said quickly. 'Well, they were all close.'

'But it's all sorted now,' Daniel continued. 'We've talked to him about it and he's on his way back to . . . Wales.'

The police officer nodded and closed his notebook. 'Give us a call if you get any more trouble,' he said to Mr Jeffries.

'I certainly will. And thanks for getting here so quickly.'

The police officer left and after a little more discussion, Emma and Daniel went too, after quietly reminding Rhydian that he was due to join the family later that evening to be with them through the night of full moon.

But Rhydian could not settle through the rest of the school day, with his usual anticipation of the coming full moon deserting him.

'What's wrong?' Maddy asked when they were alone.

'I'm worried about him; Alric.'

'Alric! Why should you worry about him?'

'I can't get the look on his face out of my head,' Rhydian said sadly.

Maddy was not sympathetic. 'He was going to kill me, Rhydian, and you too!'

'And he's lost everything, Mads.'

'And he deserved it.'

'But I really hurt him.'

'Yeah, maybe, but it was his fault and it's done now, finished.' Maddy looked closely at Rhydian. 'Just leave it at that, right?'

But Rhydian could not leave it at that; he could not leave it at all. When school was over he slipped quickly away, without a word to Maddy, sensing exactly where he needed to go and what he needed to do before joining his pack for the night of full moon.

His senses were right. Before Rhydian reached the battered old caravan, he knew that Alric was inside. He edged cautiously forward, knowing that he had to go in and face his old enemy.

Alric was leafing vacantly through one of Jana's old school books. He looked shattered and did not even glance up as Rhydian stepped into the caravan.

'For thousands of years, we've lived wild,' he muttered. 'Free. But now the light fades, and the wild with it. And all the while humans strengthen.'

187

'We're half human, too,' Rhydian said.

Alric looked up and studied Rhydian for long moments. 'You sound like her. Or perhaps she sounded like you.'

'She loved all this,' Rhydian said, glancing around the caravan. 'It was her own little world.'

'The wild is a Wolfblood's world, yet every day the human world grows. I cannot love that world, I will not.'

'But no one's trying to make you love it; you can live how you want.'

Alric sighed deeply as the memories of the last days and weeks returned. 'The wild packs that remain will not welcome an alpha in exile.'

'Then don't join a pack.'

'No Wolfblood survives alone.'

Rhydian paused before replying. 'I did.'

Alric looked at the younger Wolfblood again, seeing him differently at last and not as an enemy to be feared and hated.

'I thought I'd be on my own for my whole life,' Rhydian continued. 'But my pack found me, now it's the only pack I want. Being alone is hard but it's a fresh start, and you don't know what's gonna happen or who you'll meet. But if I can survive it, Alric, you definitely can.'

Alric said nothing but seemed to be considering Rhydian's words. Then he got quickly to his feet and Rhydian took a step back, thinking that perhaps he had said too much.

'Thank you,' Alric told him, staring into his eyes. 'Thank you, Rhydian. I will heed your words; I will start again. On my own.'

Rhydian nodded, relief flooding through his body.

'Tonight is a full moon,' Alric looked out at the darkening sky, 'my first as a lone wolf. What will you do?'

'I'll be with my pack.'

Alric nodded. 'Good luck.'

'You too.'

When Rhydian joined Maddy and her parents a little later he felt completely relaxed and at ease, ready not just for the night of full moon, but also for a peaceful and more settled future.

But as the pack went down into the den and transformed into wolves they had no idea that their whole world would very soon be shattered and changed forever.

Twenty-five

Liam, Jimi and Sam had climbed carefully down into the ancient Wolfblood lair. It was dark but Liam had planned the expedition carefully, bringing with him hard hats, protective vests and head torches for them all.

And when they gazed around the main chamber, with the fallen beams and rocks and a tunnel leading away into darkness, Jimi and Sam were suddenly struck with the realisation that perhaps, after all, there might just be something in Liam's wild claims.

Liam pointed to the tunnel. 'That is exactly where I saw the werewolf. And Maddy.'

'After you then, Wolf-man,' Jimi said. But this time the tone of his voice was not as mocking as it had been earlier in the day.

They donned the vests and fixed the torches to their hard hats so that their hands were free, and then Liam got on his knees to lead their way, squeezing into the tunnel, with Jimi and Sam following.

It was a tight fit, and the narrow tunnel seemed to

stretch on for much further than they could have imagined. But solid timbers shored up the sides and roof, so at first it felt safe enough.

The air was thick and dusty and strange sounds seemed to echo from the depths of the earth. Liam, in the lead, was as nervous as his two friends, but was determined not to show any fear.

As the tunnel narrowed even more he bumped against a side beam and a small fall of mud and earth filled their mouths and nostrils with dust.

'This is crazy!' Sam shouted from the rear. 'We should go back.'

'No! It gets wider up ahead. I can see it.'

Liam was right. They crawled wearily into a wider chamber with another tunnel on the far side. The darkness was intense and inky black. Their knees hurt and their throats were dry and what had seemed like a good idea at the beginning now felt like madness.

All three were scared, but only Sam was prepared to admit it. 'We should go turn around. We're gonna die down here.'

'Don't be stupid!' Liam snapped. 'We have to go on. There'll be another way out, there has to be; there's always two ways in and out of these tunnels. We have to go on.'

They pressed forward into the next tunnel, which was wider, with a reassuringly higher roof.

Suddenly a long howl echoed through the tunnels, and then another, followed by a third and a fourth.

The boys froze.

'Werewolves,' Liam breathed. 'I told you; I told you!'

'We have to go back.' Sam was almost in tears. 'Liam, my torch has given up. I can't see.'

'Use your phone,' Liam said as he crawled forward and Jimi followed.

'Wait for me!' Sam cried, scrabbling to use the light of his torch. 'Wait for me!'

They scrambled into a large chamber, high enough for them to at last get to their feet and stretch their aching limbs. Directly in front of them was a solid mud wall but to one side was another tunnel.

'Is this where the werewolf is?' Sam asked, his eyes wide with fear.

The howling had stopped.

'You heard them,' Liam breathed. 'We all heard them.'

'Yeah, but let's go back.'

'Go back where?' Jimi said angrily. 'We've gone miles; we've no idea where we are. We're lost.' He glared at Liam. 'I knew this was a terrible idea.'

Sam was holding up his phone to increase the light.

192

'I've got Wi-Fi,' he said, gazing at the phone's screen.

'Great,' Jimi growled. 'We'll send an email asking for help.'

'We must be near a building.'

'He's right,' Liam said urgently. 'We have to be.' He led the way into the next tunnel. It was narrow but high and at the far end was a mud wall from which a tiny chink of light shone.

'Look,' Liam whispered. 'There must be something behind there.' He reached up towards the light and brushed at the mud, which was dry and crumbly and fell away easily to reveal a small section of brickwork. The light was shining from a crack in the cement between the brickwork.

'It's a wall,' Sam gasped.

'Hello?' Liam called hesitantly.

There was no response, so Liam began to push at the brickwork. One brick was loose and it fell inwards and a weak, silvery beam, like moonlight, slid into the gloom of the tunnel.

'Anyone there?' Jimi said hesitantly.

There was no response.

'Hello?' Liam said.

A low growl came from the other side of the wall.

'What . . . what was that?' Sam whispered.

Liam leaned closer to the hole in the wall and saw the room beyond. He took his own phone and, using the camera, began filming as he attempted to push away more of the brickwork to get a better view.

Suddenly a wolf leapt up, barking ferociously and snapping at Liam's hand. He yelled in terror and pulled his bloodied fingers away from the wall.

'Run!' he screamed. 'Run!'

The Wolfbloods spent a fretful and restless night and it was only when first light came and they transformed back to human form that they could investigate further.

The brickwork inside the den had been covered with dried mud for centuries, leading Daniel to believe that behind it was nothing but solid stone. But he fetched a sledgehammer from the shed and had soon smashed down a large enough section of brickwork to allow him to get through into the tunnel.

Maddy wanted to go with him as she peered into the gloom and glimpsed the wooden support beams.

'It's like the den at Aern Hollow,' she told her dad.

'Maybe it leads there,' Rhydian said.

'I'll take a look,' Daniel told them. 'You stay in the den.'

Carrying a torch, Daniel disappeared into the darkness while the rest of the pack waited anxiously.

'I can still smell their presence,' Emma said. 'Poisoning our atmosphere.'

'It might not be as bad as we think,' Maddy said.

Rhydian was trying to be positive too. 'If they came all this way underground, they might not have a clue where they ended up.'

'They saw you, Maddy,' Emma said, staring at her daughter. 'In wolf form. It doesn't get any worse than that.'

Twenty-six

Their first instinct was to flee, disappear without trace while they could. But they had to know exactly what damage had been done before taking that ultimate step. There was still a faint hope that they might bluff it out.

Maddy and Rhydian went to school, fearing the worst, which looked like being confirmed as soon as they walked into their registration classroom.

Liam was the centre of attention, or at least, his phone was. Despite the sheer panic and terror down in the tunnel, he had managed to film perfectly the moment the wolf leapt up and snapped at his hand.

The whole class was clustered around as the clip was played over and over. Tom and Shannon came over to Maddy and Rhydian.

'What are they saying?' Maddy whispered.

'There's a werewolf in Stoneybridge!' Jimi shouted to them before Shannon could answer. He pointed at Shannon. 'Just like she always said.'

'I never said it was a werewolf!' Shannon said quickly.

'You never knew what your beast was! Now we do!
Play it again, Liam.'

Liam replayed the clip and held up the phone so that
Maddy and Rhydian could see it. It didn't make good
watching.

'It's a husky,' Rhydian said, trying to act unconcerned.
'Something like that.'

'That's not a dog! Look at it!'

'Where was this? Maddy said.

Jimi and Sam had regained their bravado. 'In the
tunnels! We went there last night.'

'Followed them for miles.'

'And that's where this thing was. At the end?'

'In some cellar.'

Liam was staring at Maddy. 'It looked like a cellar,
anyway.'

'But where exactly was it?' Rhydian asked.

Jimi shrugged. 'How are we supposed to know? It
was dark.'

The Three Ks were fascinated by the tale. 'Maybe
that's why you never found your beast, Shannon,' Katrina
said. 'It lives underground.'

Liam was still watching Maddy closely. 'But only on
a full moon. The rest of the time it lives among us – as
a human.'

Maddy felt Liam's eyes burning into her, but she said nothing.

Liam was more certain than ever that he was close to revealing the truth about the werewolf in their midst. But he had been ridiculed before and wanted to get absolute confirmation from an official source. By morning break he had emailed the film clip to Dr Whitewood, the forensic scientist who examined the Wolfblood bones discovered in the field, before they were stolen away. And as well as the clip he sent over a photo of the bite marks on his fingers.

But when they spoke on the phone, Dr Whitewood was not completely convinced. 'Well, it certainly looks canine,' she said after watching the film clip. 'But I can't be certain that it's a wolf.'

'What about the bite?' Liam asked. 'What about DNA?'

'I'm sorry, Liam, the chances of a bite like this leaving DNA in the wound are virtually nil. I need something more tangible. The animal's blood, or something with its saliva on.'

The pack gathered that evening to discuss the way forward. Daniel had been underground during the day and had made rough drawings of the network of tunnels and chambers.

'I think they're medieval,' he told everyone gathered around the table, 'from when our pack would have been wild. It's brilliant, a network of secret tunnels to hide Wolfbloods from the humans.'

'But it hasn't hidden us this time, has it?' Emma said dejectedly as she got up to make tea.

'So what do we do about Liam?' Maddy said gloomily.

No one seemed to have any ideas until Shannon spoke. 'Occam's razor.'

'What?'

Tom nodded as he recalled a previous conversation with Shannon. 'The simplest answer is usually the right one.'

'Exactly,' Shannon said, looking at Maddy. 'So we do with Liam what you did with Tom and me, we invite him into the pack.'

Rhydian shook his head. 'No, he's not pack material.'

'How do you know?'

'Instinct. I trust you and Tom, I don't trust him.'

The kettle was beginning to boil but Emma ignored it. She lifted her head and sniffed the air, and suddenly Maddy and Rhydian were doing the same.

'He's back,' Emma gasped.

They all leapt to their feet and hurtled across the room and down the stone steps to the cellar.

Liam stood in the middle of the den, his phone in one hand and a clear plastic bag containing something in the other. He had been filming and quietly recording everything in sight. And in the seconds before he heard footsteps on the stairs he had spotted a dog chew still moist with saliva on the ground, picked it up and shoved it into the bag.

'What are you doing here?' Maddy screamed furiously.

Liam didn't answer; he couldn't speak. He just gawped, thinking now that every one of them, Maddy, Rhydian, Maddy's parents, Tom and Shannon, might be were-wolves.

'Get out!' Daniel yelled. 'Get out, or I call the police! Did you hear me?'

Liam stood rooted to the spot, his eyes wide, staring from one person to the next. Finally, he managed to find his voice. 'I . . . I know *what* you are. All of you.'

Clutching his phone and the plastic bag he turned and ran back into the tunnels.

'Liam, wait!' Shannon shouted. 'I can explain! Please listen to me!'

But Liam did not stop. They heard him scrabbling away.

'Should I go after him?' Daniel said to Emma.

'And do what? Kidnap him? We have to leave. Now!'

'No, Mam, we can't just run.' Maddy was close to tears. 'He can't prove anything yet.'

'Get packing, Maddy!'

'But what about Rhydian?'

'You have to think of the family first,' Rhydian said. 'I've always got the wild pack.'

'Tom and Shannon, then?' Maddy said desperately. 'He thinks they're werewolves, too. We can't just leave them to deal with this.'

'We don't have a choice any more.'

'But we do! There is a way!'

Everyone looked at Maddy, waiting for her to speak.

'Well?' Emma asked.

'Occam's razor, like Tom and Shannon told us. The simplest answer is usually the right one. And we have to try it, Mam, we have to.'

Twenty-seven

It was a last desperate gamble, the only option left apart from running away. So they took it. Daniel phoned Mr Jeffries first thing the following morning and explained what they wanted to do at school that day. The teacher was stunned but then fascinated, and eventually agreed.

The year group were continuing with their English speaking presentations and another lesson had been arranged for the final few speakers that morning.

Rhydian sat in the hall with Tom and Shannon. Liam was doing his best to ignore them and was across the room with his friends. His phone, complete with the newly filmed evidence, was safely in his pocket and he was just waiting for the right moment to reveal all.

Miss Fitzgerald was about to start the lesson when Mr Jeffries walked in. 'I'll be sitting in on the first presentation, if that's OK with you, Miss Fitzgerald?'

'Yes, that's fine,' Miss Fitzgerald replied, looking slightly surprised. She watched as the head of year fixed the double doors open. He walked to the stage and they spoke quietly for a few moments. Miss Fitzgerald's look of surprise slowly turned to one of amazement.

Mr Jeffries turned to address the students. 'We've changed the order of today's oral presentations. Maddy Smith will go first.'

'She's not even here,' Jimi Chen muttered.

'Oh, she's here, Jimi,' Mr Jeffries replied, smiling. 'But we'll need complete silence throughout her talk. No loud noises or sudden movements, please.'

Everyone but Rhydian, Tom and Shannon sat up in their seats, suddenly intrigued to know what was going on.

'Over to you, Maddy,' Mr Jeffries called from the stage.

There were footsteps and everyone turned to see Maddy enter the hall. She stood perfectly still in the doorway, raised both her arms and clicked her fingers.

A chorus of shocked gasps ran through the onlookers as two, fully grown wolves trotted through the doorway and sat obediently on either side of Maddy.

Liam looked stunned as Maddy walked calmly to the stage with wolf-Daniel and wolf-Emma at her heels. She climbed the steps, clicked her fingers, and the wolves sat, calmly facing their audience.

Maddy smiled. 'I've been hearing a lot about were-wolves recently. But today is not a full moon, and as you can see, these are not werewolves; they're wolves, and our family pets. They're a pair of domesticated timber wolves. You need a special licence to keep them so they don't go off our land very often; farmers tend to get a bit jumpy when they see a wolf.' She paused and looked deliberately at Liam. 'And not just farmers!'

A ripple of laughter ran through the room, the mood was changing by the second. All talk and thoughts of werewolves had vanished; now there were only excited whispers as everyone gazed in awe at the two magnificent creatures sitting calmly before them.

'Our wolves are tame and friendly,' Maddy continued, her confidence growing. 'But some people hate wolves, so we keep them secret to keep them safe. That's why only our family and a few close friends know about them.'

Some of the students looked enviously towards Rhydian, Tom and Shannon, who were basking in the glory of being recognised now as that chosen few. But Liam looked devastated; his whole theory had been shot down.

'The wolves live in an old cave under our house that was built more than three hundred years ago,' Maddy went on. 'They're not used to bright lights or large crowds, so please don't try to pet them or shine lights, or take photos. They can get angry.' She smiled again, convinced that the doubters had been won over. 'So, any questions?'

A sea of hands shot into the air.

The wolves were the talk of the entire school. Even when Daniel and Emma had safely retransformed in a quiet spot and driven off in the Land Rover, the excited conversations about the incredible event continued all morning and on into the lunch break.

Only Liam, sitting alone in the playground, looked absolutely miserable. Shannon spotted him and knew from her own experiences exactly how he was feeling. She went over to speak to him. 'Not much fun, is it? Being on the receiving end of all the taunts and jokes?'

'You don't have to rub it in.'

'I'm not; really I'm not. I just mean I know what it's like. And you were brave, sticking to your story when no one believed you.'

'Didn't get me anywhere though, did it?'

'Well, they weren't werewolves after all, but there were wolves, so you're kind of half right.'

'Half an idiot, you mean.' He sighed. 'Everyone laughed at you and your beast of the moors story, but . . . well, you're all right now, aren't you?'

'Yeah,' Shannon said, smiling. 'And you'll be all right too.'

Rhydian was buzzing as he strode into the playground, thrilled that everything had worked out after all. And he wanted to celebrate. 'You're a genius,' he said excitedly to Maddy. 'You know that, don't you?'

'I suppose I do,' Maddy answered, grinning.

'So . . .' Rhydian continued, a little less confidently now, '. . . to celebrate, I was wondering if you fancy doing something tonight, going somewhere? Not Bernie's, somewhere special?'

'Rhydian, are you . . . are you asking me out on a date?'

'Well . . . you don't have to . . .' Rhydian was blushing. 'Not if you don't want to. It's up to you.'

Maddy smiled. 'Well, if it's up to me . . . I'd love to.'

Maddy was so excited when she arrived home. She was planning on taking her time in choosing an outfit to wear and getting ready to meet Rhydian. She dashed into the kitchen, bursting to speak to her parents. 'Guess what? I've got a . . .'

She stopped and stared. Sitting at the kitchen table with her ashen-faced mum and dad was the forensic scientist, Dr Whitewood, who was holding a computer printout.

Dr Whitewood smiled. 'Hello, Maddy, do come and join us.'

Maddy looked at her mum, who just nodded.

'As I was saying, the DNA results are absolutely clear,' Dr Whitewood said to Daniel and Emma as Maddy slumped down into a chair.

'From a dog chew, bitten by a wolf and handled by me,' Daniel said half-heartedly. Maddy thought her dad looked beaten, as though he had already given up the battle.

And the scientist went on with absolute conviction. 'There's no cross-contamination here, Mr Smith. The saliva on the dog chew comes from a hybrid species; part human, part wolf.' Her tone became gentle and persuasive. 'Look, all I want is the opportunity to study you, the whole family. Properly. Scientifically.'

'And what will you do about Liam?' Maddy said, unable to stay quiet.

'I'll tell Liam the chew belonged to your . . . wolves . . . and you can carry on as normal. The dog chew is quite safe in my laboratory at the university. No one but me knows the truth. And I'll keep it that way.'

'Carry on as normal?' Emma said. 'I don't think so. You want us to be your personal lab rats. I'd like you to leave.'

But Dr Whitewood was not going to give up. 'You

know, the fact that this evidence came to me first is fortunate for you. In the wrong hands . . . well, not everyone might be so reasonable.'

Emma's eyes narrowed. 'Are you threatening us?'

The scientist got to her feet. 'I just want to make sure we all know where we stand.' She reached into her coat pocket, took out a business card and placed it on the table. 'Call me when you've had a chance to think.'

Twenty-eight

Rhydian had made up his mind. There was still something he could do that might save Maddy and her family, and he was absolutely determined to do it.

Maddy had told him tearfully on the phone that Dr Whitewood had learned their secret from the saliva on the dog chew. The dog chew was in her laboratory at the university and Rhydian was going to get it to destroy the evidence. Then it would be nothing more than her word against theirs.

He'd run, all the way, across country at Wolfblood speed until he reached the Northumberland University campus, which sat in large open grounds.

No one took much notice of another young man wandering about the campus. He followed the signs for the Department of Natural Sciences and slipped into the modern, glass-fronted building without being questioned. Dr Whitewood's laboratory was listed on a noticeboard.

As he strode along a corridor, trying to look as though

he knew exactly where he was going, Rhydian realised that there was just one big difference between him and most of the students in the building – a white lab coat. He had to get one to fit in.

He passed a row of lockers and next to them was a line of coat pegs filled with jackets, duffel coats, university scarves – and a solitary white lab coat. Rhydian lifted the coat from the peg and slipped it on without even breaking his stride.

He followed the signs; Dr Whitewood's lab was on the next floor.

They were leaving; there was no longer any doubt. The only question remaining was where they would go.

'We can join Mike and Laura's pack in Devon,' Emma said as she prepared to pack suitcases. 'They've always said we could go to them if it ever came to an emergency.'

Daniel looked devastated. 'How long has our pack been here in Stoneybridge? Six hundred years? Seven? A thousand? And we'll be the ones who finally leave.'

'I'm sorry,' Maddy told them both, 'I know this is all my fault.'

'Don't you ever say that, Mads,' her mum said. 'The world's closing in on us, that's all, and there's nothing we can do about it.'

'Maybe if we got that dog chew back . . .'

Daniel shook his head. 'Devon, Scotland, she won't stop coming after us. We'll never stop running now.'

'Then we'll have to disappear.'

'What?'

Maddy looked from one parent to the other. 'Where's the one place no one could ever find us?'

'You mean . . . the wild pack?' Daniel asked.

'Us?' Emma said, dismissively. 'In the wild? We wouldn't last five minutes.'

'We would,' Maddy said. 'And with Jana in charge we'd be safe. We could learn to survive; Rhydian did.'

'For three months.'

'That was because of Alric; it's different now.'

Daniel was thinking. 'And it would give us time to make plans.'

'I don't know,' Emma said. 'I don't know.'

Maddy reached for her phone. 'I have to speak to Tom and Shannon. And Rhydian.'

A number of students were working at benches in the large laboratory when Rhydian walked in. They all seemed in their own little scientific worlds, working diligently, paying no attention to anyone else, which was fortunate for Rhydian.

The room was wide and brightly lit with three long rows of workbenches. But there was no clue at all to where the dog chew might be. Rhydian had to use his Wolfblood senses to try to pick up a scent. He sniffed the air.

A door at the far end of the room opened and Dr Whitewood emerged, carrying a clipboard, from what appeared to be her office. She was reading something attached to the board as she went over to a couple of students working together. Rhydian ducked behind a bench, relieved not to have been spotted and questioned.

He edged his way along the tiled floor, keeping his head below the level of the workbenches. Soon he could see into the room Dr Whitewood had vacated and there in the only glass jar on a shelf behind a desk, rested the dog chew, displayed like some sort of trophy.

Rhydian realised that if he was going to get it, he had to create a diversion. He reached up and took a glass, measuring vessel from the workbench and then hurled it low across the room, behind where he was hiding.

One of the students screamed in fright and everyone turned to look.

'What happened?' Dr Whitewood asked the closest student. He shook his head, and they all trooped down the room, passing the hidden Rhydian, to investigate. He had to take his chance while he could. He sprinted

212

to the office, lifted the dog chew from the glass jar and stuffed it into his mouth.

Out in the main room, Dr Whitewood was ensuring that the broken glass was properly cleared up when she spotted someone she didn't recognise hurrying from her office. 'Who's that?' she called.

Rhydian kept his head down and left the room. The scientist rushed to her office and immediately noticed the empty jar. 'No!' she yelled, turning to give chase. But by the time she reached the corridor the unfamiliar stranger was nowhere to be seen.

Rhydian was outside, running hard, veining and yellow-eyed as he munched determinedly on the dog chew. If it meant wolfing out to get rid of the evidence then he would. He stopped at a large industrial waste bin, tore off the lab coat and jammed it into the bin.

He kept chewing and chewing and then finally, he swallowed.

Twenty-nine

From the moment he saw them, Rhydian realised it was all over. They looked pale, bewildered, lost and afraid.

'But it's all right,' he said before any of the Smiths had even spoken. 'I got it, the dog chew.' He patted his stomach. 'I've eaten it. She's got no evidence any more, and without the evidence . . .'

'It's too late, Rhydian,' Daniel said simply.

Rhydian could hardly believe what he was hearing. 'But why?'

'It was too late before you even tried,' Maddy said. 'She knows about us now. Anything we've drunk out of, anything we've touched, she can get more DNA from. It would only be a matter of time.'

'We're going to the wild pack, Rhydian,' Emma said, 'it's the only safe place left for us.'

They were outside the house, the house that had been the Smith family home for hundreds of years. Now they were about to leave it forever, with nothing. No reminders, no keepsakes, no possessions at all. As wild Wolfbloods they would live and travel with only the clothes they stood up in.

Rhydian had heard Maddy's voicemail message saying that she needed to see him urgently as he ran back from the university. He'd expected a joyful reunion, a celebration with the family, and then he and Maddy alone on their date. But now they were all leaving the house for the last time.

'I can't look at it any more,' Daniel said, turning away from the ancient stone building.

They walked upwards through the trees without looking back; looking back would be too painful. They were heading towards the ridge of hills above Stoneybridge, where Maddy had arranged to meet Tom and Shannon.

Maddy and Rhydian were holding hands, they had walked in silence, both with so much to say but unable to find the words.

They waited and soon saw Tom and Shannon struggling up the steep hill towards them.

Maddy turned to Rhydian. 'Come with us? There'll be Jana, your mum, and we won't be in the wild forever.'

Rhydian had been waiting for the question from the moment he heard that they were going to the wild pack. He'd almost said instantly that he would return to the wilderness with them. But he had been thinking as he walked, his mind in turmoil.

'Maddy, I can't go with you,' he said gently. 'If you leave, it's only Whitewood looking for you. If I disappear, suddenly there's a manhunt. The Smith family kidnap a minor; it's headlines stuff. And nowhere's safe from that. I've got to stay, Maddy, for all our sakes.'

Maddy felt as though her heart was being split in two. 'Please . . .'

'He's right, Maddy,' Emma said. 'They'd hunt us down. This way we have a chance.'

Tom and Shannon finally reached them, panting and gasping for breath.

'This can't be happening,' Tom said.

'Please?' Shannon gasped. 'Please tell us you've found a way out of this?'

But there was no way out. The only way was to leave, and quickly, as the sun was setting and the sky rapidly darkening.

They moved to the top of the ridge, the place where they were to part. Beyond lay the moors, and the wilderness, beckoning, calling them home.

Maddy hugged her two childhood friends so tightly she felt they might break, just like her own heart seemed to be breaking. There were tears in all their eyes.

'Doctor Whitewood will come for you next,' Maddy said. 'Asking questions.'

'We'll defend you,' Tom said. 'Always.'

'No. You have to tell her, and tell everyone, that you were conned too. Say you thought we kept wolves.'

'But that's a betrayal, Mads,' Shannon said, tears streaming down her face.

'It'll keep you safe . . . safer. And we'll be safe too. Promise me you'll do that.'

They knew she was right -- they knew it was the only way – and they both nodded.

'And remember,' Maddy said, trying to smile, 'wherever we are, wherever you go, we'll always be a pack,' she put her hand to her chest, over her heart, 'in here.'

'Mads,' Daniel said softly, reminding her that it really was time to leave while they could.

Maddy nodded and went to Rhydian. They held hands and looked deeply into each other's eyes.

Rhydian somehow mustered a smile. 'Some date this turned out to be.'

Despite her heartbreak, Maddy laughed. She moved closer and spoke softly. 'I love you.'

And then they kissed. For the first time, for the only time.

'I love you too,' Rhydian whispered. 'I'll come and

217

find you. One day, when I'm older and no one cares what I do, I'll find you, Maddy.'

Maddy stepped back, holding Rhydian's hands until the last possible moment before letting go. 'We'll find each other.'

Don't miss

WOLF BLOOD

Wolves Among Us

Out now
Read on for a sneak peek . . .

One

The moon wasn't quite full yet, but it would be soon. Rhydian Morris looked up as it glinted in the clouded night sky. There was a time not long ago that he'd have been excited at the idea of wolfing out, but not any more. Not since Maddy Smith and her family had been forced to leave Stoneybridge. Now he'd have to wander the night alone, as if he was back to being a lone wolf. He'd finally found a pack, one that wanted him and that he wanted to be with, and then. . .

He felt something in his chest, a feeling too huge to fit into words.

He threw back his head and he *howled*.

Tom Okanawe and Shannon Kelly heard him. They were searching the Smiths' dark, abandoned stone house. Shannon had thought she'd seen lights driving up to it, but there was nothing here.

'Poor Rhydian,' she sighed, as the lonely sound of howling drifted to them again.

'It's all right for *him*,' said Tom, with a flash of annoyance, 'wolfing out on the moors.'

Shannon sighed. 'Tom, we all miss her. Come on. Let's go home.'

Shannon turned around and the light from her torch cut across the room. They both jumped out of their skins as a face stared back at them through the window. They rushed outside, but the woman had gone.

The thing about being in on the secret about Wolfbloods, Shannon thought the next morning, was that everything else seemed pretty silly, really. Take, for example, the three Ks' latest scheme. Katrina's family had bought Bernie's place and had turned it into a diner where all three girls would work. They had even asked Shannon to sing on the opening night. Her boyfriend, Harry Averwood, was going to play guitar.

Boyfriend. Shannon made a face. Even thinking the word was weird. Anyway, there were far more important things to worry about. She and Tom waited for Rhydian and then bundled him into the photography club's darkroom to tell him what they had seen the previous night.

'It was definitely Doctor Whitewood,' said Tom.

'Why come back now?' Shannon wondered. The last time they had encountered the woman, she'd managed to get hold of some of Maddy's DNA. She was the reason the Smiths had fled Stoneybridge. That was two months ago now.

'Well, she won't find any more DNA,' said Tom. 'We've scrubbed that house clean.'

'As long as she's only looking for the Smiths, you'll be safe,' Shannon told Rhydian, although he didn't seem to be listening at all.

'Shouldn't you be bouncing off the walls?' Tom asked. 'It being almost full moon, and all?'

Rhydian frowned. 'I'm fine,' he said, even though they all knew he wasn't.

'You've told Mrs Vaughn you're staying at Tom's tonight, right?' Shannon asked.

'Yeah,' Rhydian muttered, heading out of the door. Tom and Shannon followed.

'You'll need to be careful if Whitewood's on the prowl,' Shannon warned Rhydian. 'Just get as far away from Stoneybridge as you can.'

Rhydian still didn't seem to be listening. Mr Jefferies appeared, hustling everyone into the classroom. 'Come on, you lot! Hope you haven't forgotten what day it is?'

'Course not, sir,' said Katrina brightly. 'It's opening night! Drinks and live music from Shannon and Harry at the Kafe!'

'The . . . *Kafe*?' Jeffries repeated, pronouncing the name the same way Katrina had, as if it rhymed with 'safe'.

'With a K,' Katrina explained proudly. 'My idea.'

'Well, that's very creative, Katrina, but I was actually talking about the Careers Fair today. With a C.'

The Careers Fair was being held in the school hall. Rhydian really couldn't be bothered with any of it, and he wasn't the only one. Jimi Chen and Liam Hunter couldn't see the point either – Liam because he'd already decided he'd be working on the farm with his dad and Jimi because he only wanted to work for himself.

'Working for anyone else is a chumps game,' he declared. 'I'll be a millionaire before I'm twenty-five.'

'Depressing thing is he probably will be,' Shannon muttered, as Rhydian opened the door to the hall.

Rhydian froze. There was another Wolfblood here. He could *smell* them.

'Rhydian?' Shannon asked. 'What is it?'

He didn't answer. Rhydian was completely focused on following the scent trail, snaking through the maze of desks and notice boards that had been set up in the hall. It led him to a smart arrangement of desks that was obviously advertising for a company involved in the big business of science and development. There were large posters of people smiling at petri dishes in meticulously clean laboratories, of engineers drilling wells in hot and dusty countries, of suited-and-booted people sitting around conference tables.

SEGOLIA said the sign.

WORKING TOGETHER FOR ALL OUR FUTURES, declared the company's slogan.

Rhydian stopped, watching the two people standing behind the desk. One was a young man wearing a suit similar to the ones in the photograph. There was nothing interesting about him – not for Rhydian, at least. But the other. . .

She was Wolfblood, but not like any he'd ever seen before. The woman looked perfect – sharp suit, gleaming hair, neat nails. He couldn't imagine her wolfing out, running through the woods just for the sheer fun of it.

The woman was talking to Kara. Rhydian tuned in to his wolf hearing and heard her say, 'We're also the leading innovator in medical and genetic research.'

'It says here you can sponsor the most promising prospects through university,' Kara said, pointing at one of the company's prospectuses.

The woman was having trouble concentrating – she knew he was watching her, and she also knew he was

Wolfblood. She sent Kara to talk to her human colleague and then turned to look at Rhydian.

'Hello, Rhydian,' she said, just loud enough for him to hear. 'Maddy says to say hi.'

Rhydian moved closer, picking up one of the Segolia brochures. The woman glanced around to make sure no one was watching and then moved to stand beside him.

'You know Maddy?'

'Yes. Her father called, said they were going into the wild. We offered them something better. My name's Dacia Turner – graduate recruiter for the Segolia Corporation. That's one of the things Segolia does. We've set up a new life for them in Canada. Once they're settled, she'll be in contact. This was an opportunity to let you know what's going on.'

Rhydian couldn't take it all in. 'Segolia? It's . . . run by Wolfbloods?'

Dacia shook her head. 'A few employees know the secret, though most don't,' she said. 'But some of our staff and several senior executives are Wolfbloods.'

Rhydian tried to imagine it, but he couldn't. 'Sat behind a desk all day . . .'

'It's not all paperwork. We protect and serve the company's interests. And our own.'

Rhydian almost laughed at that. 'What? Like a Segolia MI6?'

'If you like. Our interests are global. There's a lot of travel and the perks are great. At full moon they fly us out to Norway. In a private jet.'

'It's a bit smaller scale up here,' Rhydian told her.

'I'm looking forward to it.'

Rhydian gave her a look. 'What?'

'I've given up Norway to meet you. The least you can do is show me a full moon Stoneybridge-style.'

'Not much "style" to it,' he said, quietly. 'Just me.'

Dacia smiled gently. 'That's the best thing about this job,' she said. 'Having a pack you belong to.'

Rhydian backed away and went to find Tom and Shannon, dragging them both outside to tell them what had happened. Shortly afterwards, he almost wished he hadn't. To say that Tom and Shannon were excited would be an understatement.

'Wolfblood Incorporated! That is so cool!' Tom crowed. 'Private jets, sharp suits . . . spying!' He tried to strike a cool James Bond-style pose. 'The name's Okanawe,' he drawled. '*Tom* Okanawe.'

Shannon was just as bad. She immediately went into full-on daydream mode. 'They have a big science division? Imagine the research they must be doing! This is amazing – it's perfect for me!' She was lying on her back on one of the picnic benches on the playground, staring up at the sky. 'They probably know everything. Why exactly you are like you are. How it all works . . .' She sat up and looked at Rhydian. 'You will put in a good word for me, right? I have to work there, even if it's after university.' Shannon glanced across the playground and then scrambled off the table to hide. 'Oh no!'

Rhydian and Tom looked around, confused. Then Tom saw Harry.

'Shan,' he said. 'Are you hiding from your own boyfriend?'

Harry headed back into the school and Shannon got up. 'He wants to rehearse again,' she groaned. 'And we have bigger things going on today, right?'

Rhydian nodded. 'Yeah, actually, we have. Check it out.' He jerked his chin towards the edge of the playground. Standing there, watching, was Doctor Whitewood. He got up and began to walk towards her, but Tom and Shan stopped him.

'Go inside,' Tom told him. 'You're not on her radar. We are.'

'I'll deal with her,' Shannon promised. She left Tom and Rhydian and marched right up to Whitewood. 'Doctor Whitewood. Shall I get Mr Jeffries?'

Whitewood looked Shannon up and down with a cold smile. 'Oh, I'm fine here. Call it scientific research.'

228

Shannon snorted. 'On what, football and gossip?'

The older woman glared at her for a second before shaking her head. 'I'm disappointed in you, Shannon. You say you want to be a scientist, and yet here you are, concealing the truth. Denying the evidence.'

'You told everyone you'd found werewolves, but when it came to providing evidence, you couldn't get any,' said Shannon.

'Because you and your werewolf friends took it,' the doctor hissed. 'You could have cleared my name any time, and you chose not to. Why? Was it just to protect Maddy, or are you and your friend Tom werewolves, too?'

Before Shannon could think of an answer, Mr Jeffries appeared.

'Doctor Whitewood,' he said. 'What a surprise. Let's take this elsewhere, shall we?'

Rhydian followed as the teacher led Whitewood to his office and shut the door. Then he listened to what was going on inside.

'You can't just walk into a school like this,' Jeffries told her.

Whitewood gave a harsh laugh. 'Oh no – I might lose my job! No, wait . . . I've already lost that, along with my friends and my reputation. Remind me, Tim, what exactly have I got to lose?

Rhydian heard Jeffries sigh. 'Rebecca, you can't go on like this.'

'I had evidence,' Whitewood said, her voice flat and cold. 'It was stolen.'

'And I saw Maddy Smith with two pet timber wolves,' the teacher told her. 'No full moon. There was no magic or monsters.'

Whitewood made a frustrated sound. 'The bones we excavated didn't steal themselves! You were there, you *know* something happened! Those tunnels, Liam's video, the DNA – how much evidence do you need before you see a pattern? Or maybe you don't want to see it. Maybe you've got a reason not to?'

'Oh, for goodness' sake!' Jeffries snapped. 'Yeah – you're right. I'm a werewolf!' Jeffries made a pathetic snarling sound, which didn't even sound like a dog, let alone a wolf. There was a brief silence and then he said. 'I'm sorry. Rebecca, look, I'm sorry, I –'

Rhydian jumped away from the door as Whitewood barrelled towards it, angry and hurt.

'I feel bad,' said Shannon, once Rhydian had told them what he'd heard. 'She's desperate.'

Rhydian was not impressed. 'You're sorry for *Whitewood*?'

'Look,' said Tom, before an argument could break

out. 'Full moon is our chance to get rid of her. She thinks either we're werewolves, or that we'll lead her to some. But we'll be at the Kafe all evening.'

Shannon perked up. 'And if she doesn't see anything, she'll think Maddy's family were the only ones and leave us alone!'

'Exactly,' said Tom. 'Everything's going to be fine.'

Rhydian wasn't listening. He was looking at a text that said:

MEET B4 MOONRISE ;)
DACIA

PRESS

Thank you for choosing a Piccadilly Press book.

If you would like to know more about our authors, our books or if you'd just like to know what we're up to, you can find us online.

www.piccadillypress.co.uk

You can also find us on:

We hope to see you soon!